All it had taken was a minute

Gabe had always thought part of Josie's allure was her lack of complication. That men saw her spunk and realized she'd be fun and then gone.

But here she was, complicating his life all to hell.

He kissed her back.

He slid his hands beneath her coat, treasuring the sensual curve of her waist. He moved his fingers up her rib cage, stopping just below those voluptuous breasts.

He wanted to touch her there. He wanted to caress her to moans, then tear off her clothes and love her.

He wanted to tell her to stop looking for a father who hadn't wanted her. She had *him*. *He* loved her.

He'd protect her.

Even from himself…

Dear Reader,

This last heroine in the HEARTLAND SISTERS trilogy is my husband's favorite. Josie Blume is all tomboy, gutsy and feisty and not a lot like ultrafeminine me. I don't worry about hubby's preference, however. I think he might just see a hint of his own orneriness in Josie. And perhaps there's a smidge of me in Josie's hero, Gabe.

My favorite part of writing is the characters—always. When people ask me how I come up with different story ideas (surely they've all been done, they explain) my answer is simple: I start with two characters. We might try to put people into categories (see tomboy, above) but we are all so wonderfully different when it comes right down to it. Why else would my best friend still feel like my best friend after over thirty years? Surely I've met other only-child, Scorpio, mother-of-two intellectuals in a three-decade time span.

Maybe. But she's the only one who responds to me as she does. (Hi, Lis!)

And that's why Josie and her sisters were so much fun to write. The three siblings grew up under a special set of circumstances, without a lot of contact with the world beyond their rural Kansas home. Their personalities changed how that past affected them. Except for a common hope for a happily-ever-after, their goals were different. I hope you enjoy Josie's quest for her heart's desire.

I always enjoy hearing from readers. Write to me via my Web site at www.kaitlynrice.com.

Happy reading!

Kaitlyn Rice

THE THIRD DAUGHTER'S WISH

Kaitlyn Rice

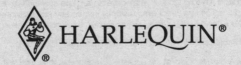

HARLEQUIN®

TORONTO • NEW YORK • LONDON
AMSTERDAM • PARIS • SYDNEY • HAMBURG
STOCKHOLM • ATHENS • TOKYO • MILAN • MADRID
PRAGUE • WARSAW • BUDAPEST • AUCKLAND

ISBN 0-373-75123-0

THE THIRD DAUGHTER'S WISH

This edition published by arrangement with Harlequin Books S.A.

® and TM are trademarks of the publisher. Trademarks indicated with
® are registered in the United States Patent and Trademark Office, the
Canadian Trade Marks Office and in other countries.

www.eHarlequin.com

Printed in U.S.A.

To my Tiger Lily cousins:
LaDonna,
Debbie,
Sheri, Karen and Joni,
Rhonda, Connie, Dani and Julie

You are all wonderfully unique, wonderfully fun. Wonderful.

Thank you for sharing yourselves, for the support, and especially for the courageous tributes you gave to my mother.

Most of all, thank you for keeping me in the loop.

Books by Kaitlyn Rice

HARLEQUIN AMERICAN ROMANCE

*Heartland Sisters

Chapter One

The man in the Wisconsin sweatshirt was eyeing Josie's butt. Gabriel Thomas was sure of it now as he watched his good friend Josie Blume approach the pool table. She analyzed the break of the pool balls, then walked around to the far corner of the barroom. She grinned when she found the angle she liked.

Glancing sideways, Gabe noted that the other man's attention shifted to Josie's chest when she leaned over the cue stick. Of course he would look there. Guys did. Despite her diminutive stature, Josie hadn't been short-changed up top. Those sexy assets curved inward to a well-toned waist, then flowed back outward to lean but feminine hips.

The woman was stacked.

She also had stylishly short brunette hair, kissably full lips and the biggest hazel eyes Gabe had ever seen. So yes, guys noticed her, Gabe included. Not that Josie would ever suspect. She thought of him as the big brother she'd never had, he was certain.

Which was for the best.

Josie must be unaware of Wisconsin's interest, or she'd have called him on the carpet for his boldness. If she was receptive to the idea of a Wednesday-night hookup, she'd have told her admirer directly that she didn't respond to drooling. If she wasn't, well, she'd have told him directly to get lost.

Josie didn't hint at what she wanted; she demanded it. And she didn't hide her thoughts behind societal expectations or womanly wiles. If you had broccoli in your teeth or conceit in your behavior, she told you about it. Yet she greeted you with such an affable enthusiasm it would be hard to dislike her, even with that sometimes blunt honesty.

Obviously, Wisconsin found her agreeable.

She should have reacted by now.

What the hey! The man's interest in Josie was no more Gabe's business than her response to it. He and Josie were merely buddies. Unless she was taking up with a conspicuous drug dealer or abusive jerk, Gabe generally kept his mouth shut about her love life.

After waiting for Josie to make a series of shots— she missed the third by a fraction of an inch—Gabe walked around to stand next to her. He lowered his mouth to her ear and murmured, "He's not your type, kid."

Josie stood up straight and looked around. "Who?"

"Wisconsin." Gabe turned to study the table. After pocketing his first solid ball, he scanned Josie's perplexed expression. "The guy behind us in the ball cap. He's enjoying those tight jeans of yours a little too much."

She scowled. "These aren't tight."

He raised his eyebrows as he perused the table again. "The outline of your driver's license is showing through your right hip pocket."

He nearly cackled when he heard the slap of her palm against her bottom.

"*You* were looking?" she asked.

Oops.

"Not in *that* way," he fibbed. As though he hadn't noticed the query in Josie's eyes, he strolled around the table and pretended to find the conversation a bore.

"I certainly hope not," she chastised. "Anyway, so what if some guy's noticing me?"

Gabe scrutinized the man against the wall behind her. After he'd bent to hit a great ricochet shot that sent his six ball into the corner pocket, he explained, "As I said before, he's not your type."

Josie stood very still, and Gabe knew she was trying not to crane her neck around to see her admirer. "I don't have a type."

"Sure, you do. This one's too young, I think."

She snorted. "If he's in Mary's Bar, he's old enough."

"*You* started sneaking in here at sixteen."

"How would you know? We met when I was *nineteen.*"

Oops again.

Gabe had heard about Josie long before the day they'd officially met. The Blume family had been different enough to cause talk, even among the Augusta cliques who considered themselves too refined for small-town Kansas gossip. Gabe's mother included.

But until he'd met Josie, Gabe had doubted the tales of little girls hiding in the attic or magazine salesmen chased off by the barrel of their mother's shotgun. Even of the boldhearted youngest daughter, who'd had the grit to defy her mother's edicts.

"We've been friends for a long time, kid," he said. "You must've told me most of your wild-and-crazy youth stories at some point." Gabe missed his next shot and moved out of her way.

Apparently, she bought his explanation. She walked around the pool table again, surveying the balls, and snuck a peek at Wisconsin on her way past.

"That guy has to be twenty-five at least," she said a few seconds later, after she'd made her shot and returned to Gabe's side. "He doesn't have a noticeable excess of tattoos or jewelry and he's gawking at me, a female, and not you, a male."

Gabe bit his tongue. Josie's standards weren't exactly celestial when it came to boyfriends. She said it all the time. The guys had to be fun, straight and un-attached. That was it, she swore.

"So he's my type," Josie said, as if Gabe had voiced some argument.

"Right, kid. If you have as few restrictions as you claim, why haven't *we* hooked up?"

Josie stared at him.

Damn it, he'd done it again. What was wrong with him? He forced a laugh. "I only meant you have more requirements than you think."

Gabe's question had bewildered him, too. The idea of hooking up with Josie sounded dangerous—and exciting. She was young, though—even younger than his twin sisters. It took on a forbidden air.

No. He wasn't the guy for Josie. Besides, if she grew bored with him in a month, as she did often with her lovers, where would their friendship stand?

Josie remained silent as she concentrated through another couple of shots, but as soon as Gabe had leaned over the table and posed his cue stick, she said, "You think you know everything about me, don't you?"

He gazed at her. "I know a few things, especially about your love life. Remember? I'm the guy you're usually with when you meet your dates."

Her eyes slid to his hairline. "Okay, do I prefer my men tall and dark or tawny and brawny?"

Gabe shot and missed. Then he made a quick study of the tuck of hair beneath Wisconsin's ball cap. Dark blond, he believed, and curly. The guy was only slightly shorter than Gabe. Josie's last boyfriend had been Hispanic. Squat and muscular, with thinning dark hair. "Guess anything goes in the looks department."

"Right. My two requirements for men are enthusiasm in bed and simplicity out of it. Commitment makes people fat and boring."

One of Josie's pet phrases.

Gabe wasn't one to question her choices. He, too, intended to lead a single life. Commitment wasn't a problem for him—it was the kids that most women set their sights on a few years down the road. A decade ago, Gabe's father had died of amyotrophic lateral sclerosis, commonly referred to as ALS or Lou Gehrig's disease, after a long and debilitating illness. Gabe couldn't risk passing on those defective genes to any male children.

But at least Gabe stayed with a woman long enough

to let her down easily when the time came. Josie tended to seek out guys who had no clue how to handle her. And she left before anyone cared.

Josie maneuvered around so her back was to Wisconsin again. Predictably, the guy leered. When Gabe caught the younger man's eye, the corners of Wisconsin's mouth twisted up in a sort of half simper, half gloat.

"Simplicity in the head, lack of skill in bed," Gabe muttered. A favorite phrase of his own, if usually unvoiced.

When Josie missed her next ball entirely and paused to glare at him, her expression was almost comically disgusted.

Her problem wasn't her pool game, however.

It was *his* big mouth.

He didn't blame her. He couldn't fathom why he was making the careless comments. Maybe because Josie had recently celebrated her twenty-seventh birthday. Their almost eight-year age difference didn't seem titanic, as it had when she was that wild nineteen and he was twenty-six.

Gabe stepped forward and sank three balls as he reminded himself that he had no business interfering in Josie's love life. No reason to warn Josie off Wisconsin.

And infinitely more reason to choke his attraction to Josie than to nurture it.

They'd ignite, explode and be done.

He liked her too much for that.

"You have to admit, the guy has a great smile," Josie said.

Gabe studied the pool table and didn't say a word.

"And if you really think I have a *type*," she added, "think about that country music deejay I dated."

"Chubby-cheeked, middle-aged wiseacre?" Gabe asked.

"Yeah." Josie nodded, lifting a corner of her mouth at some memory. "He had a *wicked* sense of humor. Man, was he fun!"

Gabe maneuvered around for a likely shot. "That guy lasted, what? Two months? One of your longer stints."

"Mmm-hmm. Now think of Jerry, the computer programmer."

Gabe hadn't liked that one, either, and Josie had dated him over the course of an entire summer.

"Remember him? *Such* an intelligent kisser."

Was she trying to prove her point, or make Gabe jealous?

"So you see?" she said. "Those two had to be total opposites. I don't have a *type*. Maybe this guy's exactly what I need to get my mind off my worries."

She swiveled to check out her admirer, dropping her scrutiny from his hat to his chest to his running shoes. Although she made a show of peering beyond him then, squinting at the clock near the bar's television, the message had been sent.

She'd looked. Briefly, but directly.

"It's getting late," she said to Gabe in an obvious tone. "Guess we should finish this game and quit."

That was when the guy approached.

Of course. Only a complete moron would have missed Josie's invitation.

Gabe frowned at the pool table as he listened to her

get-acquainted conversation with the other man. This was no big deal. Josie flirted all the time.

But tonight was a work night, and Gabe had only come out with Josie to pull her out of a blue mood. They really should be leaving soon.

After fumbling his shot, Gabe waited for a lull in the conversation so he could tell Josie it was her turn.

"I'm a student," Wisconsin was saying. "I go to Butler County Juco over in El Dorado. I was on my way home and saw this place, so…" He shrugged.

Josie had nodded through the guy's explanation. Apparently, she was still interested, even though the kid had just told her he was Juco-student age. Presumably, too young.

"Home…to Wisconsin?" Josie approached the pool table, sank her shot and then peered at the lettering on the other guy's chest.

"Nah, I bought the shirt on vacation," Wisconsin said. "I live in Wichita—Willowbend North."

The subdivision he'd named was filled with pricey homes, and no student-type rentals that Gabe could picture.

Josie let out a soft whistle. "You own a house in Willowbend?"

That grin got even more stupid. "Well, okay. I live with my parents," Wisconsin said. "But only because they're paying for my classes. As soon as I get a job that covers both rent and tuition, I'm outta there."

At least Josie was scowling now. "You don't work?"

"Sure I do. I make donuts. But my, er, responsibility eats most of my check."

Josie pocketed her last striped ball. "A responsibility besides financing your own housing?"

"A little boy," Wisconsin said. "A son. Guess he'd be about two now."

Josie gaped at the younger man. "You don't keep track of his age?"

"I don't see him all that much."

Ha! Wisconsin was starting to fidget.

"But I pay for his food and diapers. A man has to step up to the plate. I really believe that."

Gabe hid a smirk behind his beer bottle, feeling as if he'd just won some big, dopey prize at the fair. He waited while Josie missed sinking the eight ball by a mile, then stepped forward, feeling wickedly victorious as he focused again on the game.

He knew what was coming.

Wisconsin had broken Josie's biggest dating rule—and she might not acknowledge this, but she had plenty. She didn't date single dads. Under any circumstances. Ever.

"Well, good luck to you, then," Josie said as Gabe pocketed his sixth and seventh balls. "My boyfriend and I will finish this game, then get out of your way. You waiting to play, are you?"

"Your boyfriend?" Now Wisconsin gawked at Gabe. "Someone said you two were just buddies."

"You didn't ask us," Gabe said. As he had dozens of times before, he looped an arm around Josie's waist and pulled her close.

The poor guy stared, blinking a couple of times as if he was replaying Josie's earlier interest in his head. Then he met Gabe's eyes.

Gabe nodded.

"Oh, okay. Ah. I have to work in the morning. The donuts… Early." He hesitated for a second, eyeing Josie, then headed toward the exit.

"Thanks," Josie said, watching as Gabe sent the eight ball into the far corner pocket, ending their game just after she'd ended hers.

"No problem. I could tell you didn't like him all that much."

She started pulling balls from the pockets and returning them to the table. "I liked him fine until I heard about the baby he never sees."

"Nah. I don't think so." Gabe replaced the cue sticks on the wall rack. "You didn't even get his name."

Josie snorted. "Who needs a name?"

"Even you need that much, Josie. Seriously." He held her gaze.

A couple of regulars approached the table and set their beers on its edge, claiming it for the next game, so Gabe walked Josie to the parking lot.

"Sorry if I acted jerky in there," Gabe said, hoping a simple apology would work in lieu of an explanation.

"Hey, don't worry about it," she said. "That big-brother protectiveness has gotten me out of a few jams."

She always returned their status to platonic, didn't she? Except for her brothers-in-law, Gabe was the only guy Josie had been around for longer than a few months. She didn't want the complications. She said that often enough.

So Gabe would ignore the desire. Pray it abated. Maybe find a new girlfriend to distract him.

"We still on for Halloween night, then?" he asked as they approached Josie's truck.

"You bet." After opening her driver's side door, Josie reached inside the cab to grab her favorite sweater and slide into it. Then she leaned against the door frame, facing him. "I'm hunting for costume pieces this weekend. Want to come?"

"Nah. The twins helped with mine. I'm all set."

She knuckled his shoulder. "Show-off."

"Hey! I can't handle artsy on my own."

"I'll catch up with you on Halloween night then. Call me if anything changes." Her tone was affectionate, her expression soft. She'd forgiven his foolish comments.

But Josie didn't crawl into her truck. She kept leaning against it, staring past Gabe's head.

Uh-oh. Gabe recognized that expression. And he *did* know Josie. The explanation for her recent funk should spill out about…

"I think I'm going to contact my father soon."

…now.

Whoa, this one was a doozy. Josie had never met her dad. He'd left before she was born and she'd never had a clue about why or where he'd gone. The jerk had never even sent a birthday card, and he hadn't contacted the Blume sisters when their mother died.

The pain of that rejection must be the reason Josie chose the minor-league partners she did.

"Did something happen since last time you girls talked about finding him?" Gabe asked. "Wasn't that just a week ago?"

She peered at him, her eyes narrowed menacingly. "No. I haven't told them yet, so don't you go blabbing."

Gabe shot a stern look right back at her.

She sighed heavily. "Callie might believe that finding our father won't make Lilly better, but maybe if we had more information…"

The Lilly Josie was speaking about was her oldest sister Callie's six-month-old daughter. Lilly had suffered a mild, fever-related seizure at four months of age. Three weeks ago, she'd had a second, more serious, one when she was rocking in her baby swing.

The entire family had been in turmoil as the tiny girl began neurological testing.

But the sisters had discussed the idea of searching for their father. Callie felt confident that the doctors would discover the cause without an investigation of their father's genetics. She and her husband didn't have any seizure disorders, nor did any of the siblings, so Callie suspected a physiological problem.

"Didn't Callie say she thought a father search would just add stress to a tough situation?" Gabe asked.

"Mom forbade us from seeking him out. I told you that." Josie lifted a shoulder, barely. "My sisters took her more seriously than I did."

Gabe remembered Josie telling him, many times, that Ella Blume had described her husband as a weak-minded alcoholic who would taint their lives with his failures. She'd warned them to avoid contact.

Until now, they'd always heeded her advice.

Gabe also remembered pieces of gossip that gave

him an inkling about why Ella might have chosen to cut off ties to that husband—whether he was actually an alcoholic bum or some sort of blasted royalty.

However, Gabe had never found the crassness or the courage to tell Josie the things he'd heard. For one thing, he'd be repeating old gossip. And he'd discovered for himself that most of the talk about the Blume girls was simply untrue. They were a family, not a clan or a coven. Despite the unlucky circumstances of their childhood, Josie and her sisters had turned out great.

Gabe didn't want to see Josie hurt, and he feared that hurt was exactly where she was headed if she pursued contact with her father. "Josie, I think you should follow your sisters' examples and forget this. Your mom warned you that no good would come of trying to connect with your dad."

"Mother's dead."

"Haven't you always said she was very strong in her advice? Very intelligent?"

"She was also very weird."

Gabe had surmised that much.

"Don't worry about it," Josie said, before Gabe could sputter a response. "I'll keep my first few meetings with my father a secret from my sisters. At least until I feel certain that he is all right. I'd protect my family with my life, Gabe. You must see that."

Gabe did. He'd never met any siblings with a stronger bond, and that included his identical twin sisters. "If he's as bad as your mother claimed, meeting him could hurt *you*," he said.

Josie laughed. "He couldn't be any worse than the

man my mother described. If I expect a lazy bum from the outset, I can't be disappointed, right?"

No. That wasn't right. If the tales were true, she could be crushed. "Except you'll have a real image to link with her words. As it is now, you can tell yourself that this spitefulness was just another of her eccentricities."

"If we learn that he's an epileptic, we could shorten the time it takes to get answers about Lilly."

"Callie said—"

"Callie's scared and tired," Josie argued. "If I check things out before I tell her, she'll be fine." Josie wrapped her arms across her middle. "God, haven't we talked genetics a million times? You won't marry and have kids because of the Lou Gehrig's. I won't because of my mentally unstable mom. I'd have thought that you, of all people, would understand."

Ah, but there was the rub. How many times had Gabe wished he could live life normally, ignorant of the knowledge that he could pass on the gene for ALS? Had his dad foreseen his future, would he have chosen not to have kids? Was it better to know or not know?

Impossible questions, surely.

"But Lilly's already here, and so is whatever's affecting her," he said gently. "Proof that there's a genetic predisposition probably can't help now."

Josie shivered. "It's dang cold out here, Gabe. I'm sorry you don't like my idea." She hitched a breath as if she was going to say something else, but then she clamped her lips shut and climbed into her truck cab.

Gabe stepped forward so she couldn't close her door. "Have you found him already, Josie?"

She lifted her chin.

Which meant yes. She'd located her father.

"How? Through an Internet search?"

"Yep. It took some doing, but I found him, and he's not that far away," she said, sounding pleased with herself.

Damn.

"When are you going?" Gabe asked. "You said he's nearby. I'll go with you."

She sighed as she leaned backward to fish her truck key from a front pocket. "You think my old man's going to attack me?"

He rolled his eyes. "No, but you might appreciate having someone to talk to about it all. I could offer another perspective. Play that big-brother role."

She put the key in the slot, then met his gaze. "You're intense about this, Gabe. Why?"

If he told her his suspicions, he'd risk revealing secrets she might never learn for herself. Secrets best left hidden.

"You take on too much alone sometimes." He softened his voice to lessen the blow of his next words. "Shades of your mother."

"Don't worry. I'm a big girl. And you're not really my brother. Goodbye." She started her truck.

"Call me when you're going, Josie," he said over the engine noise.

She shook her head, her expression incredulous, then closed the truck door between them. She zipped out of Mary's lot and onto the street. She'd be home in two minutes.

On his sensibly slower way home, Gabe vowed to keep a close eye on Josie. They were not only friends, they were also business colleagues currently working on separate contracts within the same housing development.

He knew what she was doing a lot of the time.

Perhaps he could show up unexpectedly at her place on a regular basis and make sure she didn't meet her father on her own.

If she did it at all.

Chapter Two

Josie's truck tires spun up a cloud of dust as she traveled a lonely road in the middle of Kansas. When she approached a rise thick with spindly red cedars and yellowing cottonwoods, she spotted a mailbox tilted hopefully out toward the road. Slowing quickly, she read the boxy black numbers adhered to its side. "Nine fifty-four," she murmured, then glanced into her passenger seat to check her printout. The numbers matched. This had to be the house.

After turning into the drive, she weaved the truck through a succession of dry potholes, then parked behind a dingy white van and yanked her keys from the ignition.

Abruptly, the bold curiosity that had kept her foot heavy on the pedal from her house to this one failed. She opened the bottled soda she'd bought at a highway service station, tipped it high against her lips and winced as the soda went down. It was too warm to quench thirst. Too sugary to satisfy. Josie craved the bitter snap of a cold beer. Just one, for courage.

But she was driving and it was early—she'd had to sneak out at the crack of dawn to avoid Gabe, who'd been wanting to hang out more than usual lately. Besides, she never drank alone, thanks to a nagging worry that her taste for brew meant she was on her way to alcoholism. Like her father.

Josie had her mom to thank for most of that worry. But Ella Blume wasn't around anymore, to check Josie's refrigerator for beer bottles or her life for stray men. Despite Ella's clean, simple living, she'd died of ovarian cancer when she was barely into her fifties.

Her mother hadn't been wrong about everything, of course, but she hadn't been right about a lot. All men were not worthless. The outside world was not an evil place. Josie hoped her mother had been wrong about her father, too.

How could a man be completely uninterested in his own children? Would the knowledge that he had grandchildren draw him closer to the family? Would he be concerned about Lilly's well-being?

Josie had a thousand questions. He'd answer some of them, she was certain. After recapping the soft-drink bottle, Josie set it in her cup holder and eyed the shabby two-story a dozen yards ahead.

For some reason, she'd always envisioned her father in a sprawling ranch. This smallish house had the flat, no-nonsense lines of the Prairie-style architecture prevalent in the Midwest over a century ago.

If someone spent a little time out here with a paintbrush and hammer, the structure could be gorgeous. The patchwork yard of cracking mud and weedy, dormant grass could also use some TLC. Josie's theory about her father's destination after his departure was also wrecked. Apparently, he hadn't fled small-town life to seek fortune in some distant metropolis. Woodbine was little more than a scattering of homes. Tiny even when compared with Augusta's population of eight-thousand.

Josie wondered if her father had left Kansas and returned, or if he'd always been here—just ninety miles north of home on highway seventy-seven. Close enough to pop by once or twice in twenty-seven years to say, "Hi, I'm your dad. How are you?"

As soon as she stepped down from her truck, the sound of barking dogs caught her attention. Stuffing her key into her jeans pocket, she swiveled to peruse the end of the drive. Five or six big dogs stood enclosed in a row of chain-link pens beneath the cedars. They must have been hidden from the road.

She hadn't pictured her dad as a dog owner. Her mother hadn't allowed pets.

Perhaps the man had always wanted a dog. Maybe it was one of several things that had caused such a furious schism between husband and wife. Josie didn't know. Callie was the only one who remembered their father, but her memories were sketchy. A trip to a carnival, where their father had lifted her onto a white carousel horse. Coins emptied from his pockets and scattered on the back porch step while he taught her to count the pennies.

A man who cared for dogs now would be curious about that little girl he'd loved then, wouldn't he? He'd wonder about all three of his little girls. Even the one he'd never seen.

The pain in that thought struck. Josie couldn't decide if she was here for Lilly's sake or her own. She hesitated, motionless for a moment while she tried to decide whether to approach the house or forget it.

A breeze soothed her neck and hands, diverting her attention long enough to calm her fears. After removing her sweater, she folded it over her arm.

The worst that could happen was that her father would be the drunken fool that Ella had described. If he was, Josie would ask about any seizure disorders and go away. She hadn't driven all this way to chicken out. Not without resolving a single question.

"Here goes nothing," she muttered, and strode up the drive.

The square, concrete porch was inviting enough. Clay pots of orange chrysanthemums flanked the metal storm door, and the wooden angel plaque hanging next to it proclaimed visitors welcome in gold stenciled lettering.

Before Josie had located the doorbell, a movement in the front window caught her eye. She paused with her hand outstretched and resisted another urge to run. She had probably been seen by now, anyway.

She pressed the button, then dropped her hand and waited for someone to greet her. A single bark sounded, louder and closer than the others, but the door remained closed.

Could someone be spying on her through the window? Could *he* be watching her?

Stepping backward, she peered through a sagging set of miniblinds and caught a glimpse of a large, black nose and a wagging tail.

Her watcher was a dog. Just another dog, thank heaven. Man, she was flustered. Idly, she puzzled over why this pooch merited indoor status, when the ones out at the road were surely as lovable. And then it hit her that her father could have other children. Kids he valued more dearly, for some reason, than Josie and her sisters.

Why on earth hadn't she contacted him before making this trip?

She was impetuous, that was why. Gabe told her that often enough. But if she didn't think well on her feet, she wouldn't survive as an interior designer. Clients changed their minds all the time.

That was what she told Gabe in response to his lectures. The man drove her insane sometimes. Lord help her if he ever learned she had a thing for him. Clearly she was confusing her feelings—craving the attention of a strong man.

But Gabe was her good friend, and not boyfriend material for Josie. He *couldn't* find out about her crush. That was all there was to it.

And she'd never tell him that her mother would have agreed with him about her impulsiveness. Ella had always encouraged Josie to follow her sisters' examples, and think long and hard before she acted.

That was another reason Josie was here. Their isolated childhood had made all three of the Blume sisters feel different. Within the family, however, Josie was the only oddball. Her sisters were reserved and thoughtful; she was loud and reckless. They excelled at math and science; she'd had to work to conquer those subjects.

But whenever something in the house had broken, Josie had been the go-to girl. She didn't even look like her family. They were tall, slim and fair-skinned. She was short, buxom and dark.

Did she take after her father? Did she act like him?

She'd sought out her father for Lilly's sake. Truly she had. But Josie was also here for herself.

She wouldn't bother with ringing the doorbell again. The dog stood at the window, wagging tongue and tail, but there were no noises from within. Obviously, no one was home.

Josie was both disappointed and relieved. As she returned to her truck, she determined to follow proper procedures the next time she attempted to meet her father. *If* she tried again. She'd send a letter and follow it up with a phone call.

The outside dogs started a frenzied round of barking that caused Josie to glance toward the road. A shiny red pickup had just pulled into the drive.

Oh, God. That must be him. Man, she was scared!

Clutching her sweater to her chest, Josie watched the pickup window. A sober-faced man lifted a hand off his steering wheel in greeting, then the woman passenger waved, too.

Her father had never divorced her mother, so new questions arose.

In that instant, Josie envisioned how tough it would be to approach that front porch Welcome sign and announce, "Hi, Dad and Whoever. I'm the daughter you never bothered to meet. Aren't I clever to look you up? Now, let's discuss your health."

Maybe such a jarring proclamation wasn't necessary. Before she identified herself, she could acquaint herself with him in a safe way. If she offered a bogus name and reason for being there, she could simply talk to him. If he behaved decently enough, she'd tell him the truth: that she was his third daughter, here with questions about any seizure disorders.

That was plan enough for now.

The man steered the pickup to the opposite side of the drive to park, allowing her the space to get her truck turned around. The woman got out first. She was about Josie's height and stocky, with rust-colored curls and solemn brown eyes that filled the frames of her purple-rimmed glasses.

When the man stood up, Josie noticed he was very tall and thin. The woman had already climbed the porch steps, but he approached the house with a more cautious gait.

He was older than Josie had imagined—perhaps in his seventies. His blue buttoned shirt and tan pants hung loosely on a gaunt frame, and his head was saved from total baldness by a low fringe of wiry hair. He reminded her of someone…some celebrity—Art Garfunkel! Except that this man wore bifocals and his hair was snowy white.

He stopped beside the woman, peering shyly at Josie. "Gonna introduce us, Brenda?"

Josie felt a heaviness in her chest, and it took a second for her to realize the source of her disappointment. She'd hoped to have her father's eyes or his hair or his build. She'd dreamed that her father would take one look at her, recognize who she was and pull her into a hug.

She'd prayed for that easy connection.

Before the woman could announce that their visitor was a stranger to her, Josie offered her hand. "Hi, I'm Sarah. Sarah, ah, Thomas." She'd used her middle and Gabe's last names. As she turned to grasp her father's hand for the first time, she said, "If you're Roderick Blume, I'm here to see you."

Lying about her name didn't feel half as strange as saying his. Her mother had always referred to her father as him, that fool man or Rick. Josie's Internet search had been lengthened by days, until she had followed yet another wrong path and discovered she should be searching for a Roderick and not a Richard.

"I'm Rick Blume and this is Brenda," he said. "Can we help you with something?"

"Invite her inside," Brenda urged. "You're late taking your pills and I'm too hungry to keep dinner waiting tonight." After unlocking the door, she pushed it open and spoke gently to the dog as she made her way inside.

The man…Rick…*her father*—Josie wasn't even sure how to think of him—knit his brow. "You're not selling anything, are you?"

"No, I—"

"You're not from the county? The dogs get fresh water three times a day, and Brenda feeds them an expensive, high-protein food she buys online."

"I'm not here about the dogs. I'm visiting from Augusta," she said, deciding to stick to a version of the truth. "I know your relatives there."

Her father backed up a step. Josie got the impression that he'd prefer dealing with the dreaded salesperson or an animal welfare worker, rather than someone snooping around about his past. "You mean Ella?" he asked, studying Josie. "Or the girls? They'd be 'bout your age, I guess."

"All of them." Josie forced a calm expression.

Rick's eyes grew dark, and she waited patiently while he wrestled with the worries or regrets he should have dealt with a long time ago.

After a moment, he opened the door. "Down, Gracie!" he told the dog as he waved Josie inside.

Gracie sniffed Josie's hand, then trotted to a floral armchair near the window and stood, as if to communicate that this was the preferred spot for guests.

"Have a seat," Rick prompted.

She did so, folding her sweater across her lap. When Gracie sat at her feet, Josie leaned forward to rub the dog's silky ears. Her father crossed to the end of the sofa nearest the kitchen and yanked a blue tea towel from between the cushions. Bending slightly, he spread it across the worn armrest and tucked it in at the back. Then he sat down, sighed and knocked it half off again with his elbow.

He must sit in that same spot all the time. He must repeat those motions several times a day.

Questions were being answered without any need for conversation. Rick Blume was fair-skinned, cautious and methodical.

Nothing at all like her.

When Brenda returned to the living room to offer Rick

a glass of water and a handful of pills, he grinned wryly at Josie's concerned gaze. "When you get to be my age, the pharmacist has to help keep the old heart ticking."

Heart ticking. Could this problem be seizure related? And he'd been driving. Did that mean anything?

Josie hmmmed her concern, hoping to draw explanations.

"I was always strong as an ox," he said. "Years of eating fried bologna and kraut dogs gave me a heart attack coupla years ago. Now I live on pills and greens."

It didn't sound as if he had a seizure disorder, but she couldn't be certain without asking specifically. Josie watched her father swallow the pills and return the glass to Brenda, and a new worry invaded her thoughts. What if the shock of learning her identity canceled the effects of those pills? What if the man died here and now? From a seizure. A heart attack. Shock.

"Would you drink some coffee or iced tea?" Brenda asked Josie on her way to the kitchen.

"No, thanks." Josie wished she could follow Brenda and escape out the back door. Her father had just said he'd always been as strong as an ox. He drove a truck. If he'd suffered from epilepsy or some other disorder, it must be well under control.

Josie's sister and brother-in-law would work until Lilly's condition was controlled or extinguished. Why disturb an old man's contented life? Perhaps Gabe and her sisters were right.

"How are they?" Rick asked, causing Josie to jump. He leaned forward on the sofa, as if eager to hear the answer.

This was her opening. *Ella died seven years ago, but*

her children are great, she might tell him. Then, *Enjoy your life.* And *Goodbye.*

"They are fine," she said. "More than fine, actually. They are amazing people."

"Are they?" He peered into Josie's eyes, nodding slowly. "Brenda's cousin read about Ella's passing in the Kansas City paper several years ago. I thought about contacting the children then, but figured I was too late."

"You did?"

He sat back in the chair, his hand trembling when he lifted it to remove his glasses. As he directed his grimace downward to rub the lenses against the tea towel, he said, "Ella didn't want me to come around and disrupt her plans for those girls, but I missed knowing them."

Whatever had happened between her parents to split them up, the man didn't act monstrous now. Perhaps he'd simply fallen victim to Mother's fierce personality, as Josie and her sisters had.

"Do you want me to tell you about them?" Josie asked.

He readjusted his glasses over his ears and nose, then stared across at her. A moment later, he gave another nod.

There was so much to tell. Josie was proud of her sisters. They were exceptional. She sometimes wondered if she'd have survived her childhood if Callie and Isabel, the middle sister, hadn't been around to buffer the experience. It would be tougher to brag about herself, but Rick's reaction to that particular description should be interesting.

"Callie's a research scientist who lives in Wichita

with her husband, Ethan," she began. "They have a kindergarten-aged boy named Luke and a baby girl named Lilly."

She might have mentioned Lilly's seizures then, but her father pulled off his glasses again. Josie realized they had fogged. He blinked a few times, then wiped his index finger against the corner of his eyes. Was their conversation affecting him? God, Josie hoped so.

"Calliope was smart as a whip," he said as he laid the wire-rimmed spectacles atop the towel. "I could tell that by the time she was old enough to talk."

His sweet, tremulous smile was encouraging. Without his glasses, she could see that his eyes were a soft gray, like Callie's, and that his eyebrows had the same wide and pleasing arch that Isabel's did.

She'd definitely found her father.

"She's still smart."

Josie remembered the billfold she kept in her truck's glove compartment. She'd crammed the accordion-style photo sleeve full of niece and nephew pictures. Should she go out and get them? Was this the right moment to tell her father the truth?

"And the youngest girl was only a tiny thing last time I saw her," her father said.

Josie thought for a moment he was speaking about her. She was about to mention the fact that he'd actually left before she was born, until he added, "She was a happy thing, with pretty blue eyes and wavy brown hair."

Josie's hair was board-straight, her eyes hazel. Her father had just described Isabel. Had he forgotten that he had another daughter? Well, he did. And right now she felt ignored, abandoned and outraged.

She should have escaped when she could.

"That little girl followed her mama around as if they were attached at the heart by a strand of Elly's yarn," Rick added. "How is she?"

"You mean Isabel?" Josie prompted.

"That's right, Isabel," he said. "I do love that name, and I got to choose it for her. What's she doing?"

"She married a Colorado law professor a couple of years ago. She and Trevor live near Boulder and have a one-year-old daughter named Darlene. Izzy works with kids at a wilderness camp, and also runs Blume-crafts. Remember their mother's business?"

"I do remember. Hard to believe the baby has a child now, too."

Josie was the baby, not Isabel. Why didn't he mention her? She worked up the guts to ask. She should just say it. *I don't take after Ella physically, but I'm just as stubborn and I, too, inherited her artistic talent.*

If Rick had made the slightest indication that he knew about and was interested in her, she might have found the courage. Or if she wasn't alone here to deal with an old man's reaction to her news.

Suddenly, she wished she'd invited Gabe. Maybe. She leaned on him enough already.

"Do those girls want to meet me?" Rick asked.

"Callie and Isabel?" Josie queried, clarifying for herself that he wasn't speaking of all three of them now. That poor health or a mixture of medicines or nervous forgetfulness hadn't caused him to omit mention of the third daughter.

"Of course. Calliope and Isabel. My children."

The rock that had lodged in Josie's chest earlier seemed to turn, piercing the tender flesh around her heart.

He *didn't* know about her. Or if he did, he'd forgotten or blocked out the memory.

What would happen if she just got up and left now, and never told a soul about her trip to Woodbine today? The thought was tempting. But her father had asked her a question, and even now those cool gray eyes sought an answer.

Did her sisters want to meet him?

No. They had made it clear that they saw no advantage to meeting their father. Despite Josie's arguments. Despite Lilly's condition. Whenever the subject came up, they both said that Ella must have had good cause to warn against the contact.

If Josie told her sisters about Rick's apparent forgetfulness concerning the third baby, they might change their minds. They might want to meet him to support Josie.

Yet to all appearances, Rick was harmless. He was just a quiet old man. And he had expressed a genuine interest, at least in them.

"Maybe they'll want to meet you," she said. "I don't know. I'll mention the idea to them."

"You do that," he said, standing. He shuffled into the hallway and rummaged around in a glass candy dish. After pulling out a business card, he returned and handed it to Josie. "This card's for Brenda's dog-breeding outfit, but the phone number's the same. Have your friends call me, er, Sarah? Sarah Thomas, didn't you say?"

She stared blankly at him until the dog cued her by trotting to the front door. "Sarah. Right," Josie said. She stuck the card in her pocket and allowed her father to let her out, then waved from her truck window before she looped out of the drive.

She hadn't even talked about Lilly's condition. She'd gotten hints that her father might not have a history of seizures, but she hadn't asked.

She'd learned a lot of other things today, however. Rick Blume was just an old man, either forgetful or ignorant of a few truths about his past. Thoughtful, in some ways. Introspective—like her sisters.

Josie preferred action. People. Noise.

The more she'd spoken to her father today, the more she'd been reminded of everyone but her. In a family of tortoises, she was the only hare.

She wanted to think for a while, to figure out how or if she should return to discuss Lilly, and if she should break the other news to her father at all.

Congratulations, you have a girl! She has brown hair and hazel eyes, and weighs a smidge over a hundred and thirty pounds.

That wouldn't be right. She also wanted to settle into her feelings before she told her sisters that she'd contacted Rick Blume. She wouldn't risk inviting the man into their lives if doing so would harm her family.

She wouldn't breathe a word about this to Gabe,

either. He'd probably just give her a hard time for not warning him about her trip to Woodbine today. And then he'd proceed to tell her exactly how she should have handled it and what she should do next. The man liked being in charge.

But then, Gabe had strong ideas about a father's role in a child's life. Real strong ideas. She couldn't fault him for feeling the way he did. His dad had been his hero.

She simply wanted to handle this in her own time, and in her own way. Keeping the secret might be hard. Josie might have invited trouble by concealing her identity, but she hadn't anticipated her father's response, or the pain she'd feel when he hadn't mentioned her.

But perhaps Rick had left the family before Josie's mother had told him about the pregnancy. Maybe there was more to their history than Josie and her sisters had realized.

Right now, Josie sensed that that was exactly the case, and that her quest for answers had just begun.

Chapter Three

Three evenings later, Josie stood in her own front doorway, chortling as Gabe reacted to her costume.

"You're going to my mom and stepdad's shindig as Doc Holliday?" he inquired through the screen.

His bewildered expression was priceless. When she'd told Gabe that she was going to tonight's costume party as Wyatt Earp's favorite sidekick, she'd known he'd make a big assumption. After all, the gunslinger's third and favorite wife had been named Josephine Sarah, like her.

She might be laughing hardest at her own joke, but Gabe wasn't exactly crying. His gaze had lingered a little too long on her flattened chest, and now he was growing an annoyingly large smirk.

"Gabe!" she scolded. "I'm dressed as a man!"

"So?"

"So stop staring at my chest!"

"Just wondering where you'd put 'em."

She glanced down at her buttoned white shirt and vest. "I wore a tight body suit underneath, that's all."

The teasing glint in his baby blues warped his look of concern. "Does it hurt?"

"Of course not."

"This party could go on until the wee hours. Who knows how you'll feel after several hours of being squashed up like that? If you want me to help unbind or…"

"Gabe!"

"Fluff or reinflate anything later, I—"

Josie slammed the solid wood door shut between them.

Gabe promptly opened it. "Sheesh!" he said, shouldering his way inside. "Can't a guy enjoy a good prank when it's played on him?"

His Ropers clunked on the threshold, and the scent that wafted in ahead of him was a pleasing mixture of worn leather and expensive male cologne. "Are you really that mad?"

"I don't get mad," she insisted, then ignored his rude snort as they stood together in the entryway.

"Now that the shock has worn off, let me take a gander." He waggled his index finger around in a circle.

Sucking her cheeks in, Josie bit down on them to exaggerate the famous dentist's hollow cheeks. She turned slowly, allowing Gabe to see her full costume. She'd found a long, gray coat at the thrift store and scrounged a pair of ancient work boots from the attic. She hadn't been able to get her hands on a wide-brimmed hat, so she'd parted and slicked down her hair in a masculine style.

Gabe shook his head. "You look like Doc Holliday."

"Now you show me."

Gabe's pivot was smooth, but he added a healthy dose of male swagger. As well he should. Tall and tanned, he had magnificent muscle tone and a face that broke hearts on a regular basis. He could probably shave a labyrinth into his golden-brown curls, leave food fragments in his straight white teeth and trade clothes with his grungiest friend, and women would still offer him paper scraps with their phone numbers. The man was a bona fide hunk.

Another thing Josie would never tell him.

"Good job," she said. "I especially like the vest and holster." She reached up to yank at a few strands of his thick mustache. "This isn't yours, is it?"

After slapping her hand away, he pressed a finger against the fake facial hair to keep it from peeling off. "Of course not. You saw me clean-shaven a couple of days ago."

"Just checking," she said, smiling as he worked to restick the edges.

He had to be sexier than the real Wyatt Earp. It might have been fun to play Josephine to his Wyatt tonight. To arrive at the party on the arm of a handsome good guy, to dance in his arms. Perhaps even enjoy a little old time smooching out behind the barn.

She couldn't do that, of course.

Josie was no fool. Her longest intimate relationship had lasted eleven weeks. Her platonic connections were much more solid. She hung out with the guys over whichever sporting event was in season, and they swapped tales of work and romance wins and woes. She liked men, and her buddies were the best of the bunch.

She didn't sleep with them, though. Sleeping with men led to departures of men. She wouldn't lose a friend that way. Especially not Gabe.

"Really thought I'd dress as your wife, huh?" she asked as she crossed her living room.

"Would it be that bad?"

"Aw heck, Gabe. You want a wife? Just empty your pants pockets before you do your laundry."

"Beg pardon?"

She laughed. "Dial the number on one of the business cards or napkin scraps you find in there." She strode into the kitchen to grab a paper bag full of plastic-wrapped marshmallow and cereal treats. "Those women aren't looking for job interviews, my friend," she hollered back.

"I'm not looking for a wife and you know it," he shouted. "I was merely surprised at your choice of costumes."

"Just admit it, I got you." She lowered her voice as she returned to Gabe to exit via the door behind him.

As if he were the real Wyatt Earp facing off some outlaw, Gabe remained in place, his hands low on his hips. "You about ready, then?" he asked when she finally stopped a short four inches from his chest.

Josie throttled a grin. She'd met Gabe when she was a college sophomore running the weekend registers at the hardware store and he was a hungry carpenter with a perpetual need for supplies. These days when the proud owner of Thomas Contracting landed jobs that required interior design work, he talked up her skills. Josie referred construction work to him.

She had a great deal of respect for Gabe's talent and integrity, but he could be too serious. Too logical. When he was in an ornery mood, though, he was more fun than anyone.

Josie craved that distraction tonight. As she looked up into his gleaming eyes, she stepped squarely on his toe. "You're the one who's not moving."

He yanked his boot from beneath hers, then swung around and offered her an elbow. She hooked a hand around it and they stepped outside. He waited on the porch while she locked her house, then offered his arm again as they approached the driveway.

Tonight should be a blast.

When Josie reached her truck, she stopped. Gabe kept going and nearly yanked her arm out of the socket.

"Ow!"

He mumbled an apology, but also untangled his arm and kept walking toward his pearl-white BMW, parked behind her truck in the drive. "We're taking my car, kid."

"Nope." She lifted her keys to jingle them. "Move the overpriced status symbol. I'm driving."

Gabe stopped and turned around near his car. He shoved his thumbs over his holster and leaned a hip against his fender, appearing as though he could wait all evening.

She sighed. He'd had that dang car just over a month. Every year when the new models came out, he traded up. She'd been driving the same Toyota pickup for ten years. It had heart, like her. Gabe's cars were simply vehicles, and she told him so, often.

After a moment, he broke their staring match to

frown down at his clothes. "I can't ride with you," he said. "I borrowed this shirt from Nadine's husband."

Nadine was Gabe's younger sister by six years, and Livy's twin. The fact that Gabe had borrowed the Western-style shirt from his brother-in-law was no great shock, but Josie couldn't fathom what he'd meant by the comment.

"These boots used to be my mother's," she said. "How would borrowed clothes factor into this decision about who drives?"

"I can't risk ruining the shirt with blood or broken glass," he said, deadpan. Then he walked around to the passenger side of his car and opened it, indicating with a nod that she should duck inside.

She stood her ground. "You're not risking anything. I'm a great driver."

"Except you rely on everyone else to be on their toes." He leaned down to pat the car seat. "Get in. We're taking the car."

She waved the paper bag. "Can't. I need to go by Callie's before the party."

"I know the way to your sister's house."

Josie scowled and kept her feet planted.

"Come on, Josie." Gabe leaned an arm across the top of his car door. "I'll be the designated driver and you can have as good a time as you want."

Now, that was tempting. A couple of beers and she'd be primed to party. Maybe she'd forget all her turmoil about her visit with her father.

"You can get completely schnockered if you like," Gabe added.

Josie didn't drink that much. She made certain she didn't. And worried anyway.

Lifting her chin, she crossed the space between her truck and Gabe's car. "For your information, I've never once been *schnockered*. I drink one or two at a time, and generally only on weekends." She slid inside and slammed the car door before Gabe could respond.

But of course, after Gabe had come around and folded his long frame behind the steering wheel, he said, "You're practically a miniature person, so two could get you into plenty of trouble."

"I'm five-four—almost average for a woman my age." She sounded huffy, but she couldn't help it. Her height, or lack of it, was also a sore point.

Gabe winked.

Ooh! The man could push her buttons! Josie opened her mouth to tell him what she thought of his teasing, but shut it again when she noticed his eyes.

His gaze had locked on her lips, and he was frowning. His mustache hopped from side to side as he wiggled his jaw. Then he pursed his lips slightly.

"Uh, Gabe? What are you doing?"

He lifted his eyes to hers. "Your mustache is crooked."

"Oh, for Pete's sake!" She felt her own pasted-on mustache and discovered one side hanging loose. "Can I borrow that?" She pointed to his rearview mirror.

"Sure."

She set the paper bag on the floorboard, then slid halfway onto his car's middle console and tilted the mirror her way.

Gabe didn't start the car. As she worked to peel off the left edge of the mustache and restick it, he sat with the full length of his leg pressed against hers.

"What are you doing now?" she asked.

"Enjoying the view."

She flicked a gaze at his muscular thighs and just higher, for an instant. "Uh-huh! You were liking more than the view."

"You're the one on my side of the car."

She bounced into her seat, returned the treat bag to her lap and stuck her tongue out at him. Then she reached up to jerk the mirror around to face him. "Yours is still loose on one side."

He flipped the visor down in front of him and used *that* mirror to adjust his costume piece.

Immediately, Josie looked behind her visor and discovered another vanity mirror there. "You should have told me," she said as she snapped it back into place. "I forget about the cushy doodads in your stuffy cars."

He didn't offer a countering response. When he finished adjusting his mustache, he turned toward her. "Better?"

His eyes held the mischievous gleam she'd seen a hundred times before, and that flash of teeth was devilish. Her heart skittered into a quicker rhythm.

Sometimes Josie wondered what it would be like to love a man like Gabe. To love a man fully. Sometimes she ached for that connection.

Gabe peered into the mirror again. "Still crooked?"

She averted her gaze. "Nope. You're fine."

"Good." She heard the flap of his visor, then he started the car and backed out of the drive.

Finally.

Josie needed to get to that party. Her only thoughts should be about having a great time and forgetting the one man in the world who could hurt her. Who *had* hurt her, whether he'd intended to or not.

That man was her father.

Certainly not Gabe Thomas.

As GABE BEGAN the thirty-minute drive from Augusta to Wichita, he and Josie talked about the party and who they might see there. About a hundred home-improvement industry professionals had been invited to the annual event thrown by Gabe's mother and step-father, who owned a big lumber-supply company in east Wichita.

True to his word, Gabe drove past the east Wichita exits, continuing on to Ethan and Callie Taylor's west-side home. By the time he approached their house, it was eight o'clock and well past dark. Yet the house behind the curtains was unlit.

"I hope everything's okay," Josie said, clicking out of her seat belt before Gabe had braked in the drive. "What if Lilly had another seizure? They could be at the hospital again."

"Don't decide that now," Gabe said as he followed Josie to the porch. "Maybe they're putting the kids to bed or sitting out in the backyard. Did they expect you?"

"Ethan's working tonight, but Callie and the kids

should be home. She'd leave the porch light on, I think."
Josie rang the bell.

Callie opened the door seconds later, calm and elegant
despite the green glitter antennae she wore atop her blond
head. "Hi, you two." She smiled tiredly as she looked
from her sister's costume to Gabe's. "How appropriate."

"Everything okay?" Josie cocked her head to peer
beyond her sister into the house.

"Sure. Things are fine."

"Your lights are out," Josie said.

"Oh. Sorry." Callie opened the screen door and
motioned them inside. "I'm trying to keep things calm
for Lilly. When I ran out of candy, I turned off the front
lights and took her and Luke back to the kitchen. I didn't
want the neighborhood kids to keep ringing the bell."

Callie led them through the house to the kitchen.
Lilly had fallen asleep in front of the bowl of Cheerios
on her high chair. Five-year-old Luke sat at the table, his
entire arm crammed inside a plastic pumpkin container.
Wordlessly, the sturdy brown-eyed boy studied Gabe
and Josie as he removed a lollipop from the pumpkin.
After he had set it with a pile of similar treats, he said,
"I didn't know grown-ups could go trick-a-treatin'."

"Gabe and I aren't trick-or-treating." Josie approached her nephew and claimed a chair next to him.
"We're on our way to a costume party."

Callie pulled her sleeping baby from the high chair.
"Lilly conked out a few minutes ago. I'll go put her in
her crib."

Josie eyed her niece, a delicate blonde dressed in a
pink bunny suit. "She's really okay? Normal?"

"Not quite normal," Callie said. "She hasn't had any other seizures, but I'm noticing some eye fluttering when she wakes up. If she has another episode, her doctor's going to give me a referral to a pediatric neurologist in Kansas City."

"Good." Josie saw that Gabe was still standing and yanked out a chair next to her. "Siddown, Gabe."

"Oh, please do!" Callie said, standing with the angelic baby at her chest. "I forget you're company. You aren't company! Be comfortable!"

As Gabe sat, Lilly made signs of rousing, so Callie glided out of the room to put her to bed.

"Can I go to the party?" Luke asked, staring at his aunt. "I ate five red taffies. Mom says no more candy, but I can probably have some cake."

"This is an adult party and you'd hate it," Josie said, grinning at Gabe. "All talk and no cake."

Luke wrinkled his nose, then picked up a piece of yellow taffy and squashed it between his fingers before sorting it into a pile. He scrutinized the badge on Gabe's vest, then asked, "You a pleece-man?"

"Sort of," Gabe said. "I'm dressed as Wyatt Earp, who was a lawman in cowboy days."

Luke's eyes widened. "Cool." Then he studied his aunt, his expression serious again. "You a cowboy pleece-man, too, Aunt Josie?"

"Yes."

"But you're a girl."

"Girls can be police officers or doctors or whatever they want to be," Josie said. "Your mother's a research scientist, right? That's a difficult and very important job."

"I know. My daddy says a girl can even be president." Luke's words made clear his belief in his father's wisdom. "But does a girl pleece-man hafta dress like a boy? A *spooky* boy?"

Gabe chuckled at Josie's gasp of offense. "She's supposed to be Doc Holliday, who was a male dentist in cowboy days," he said. "Sometimes he helped Wyatt Earp with the policing duties."

Luke studied his aunt's manly hairstyle for a moment. Finally, he gave a nod. Then he pointed proudly at his own badge. "I'm a pleece-man, too, but not a cowboy. I'm a detective like my dad. He rocks socks!"

"He is pretty great, isn't he?" Josie said.

"Yep." The little boy nodded. "Lilly can be a doctor like my mom. I wanna be a pleece-man. My teacher says I even take after Daddy!"

Josie's hazel eyes grew distant. She sat staring at Luke's candy piles.

Worrying about Lilly again, probably.

Gabe contemplated Luke's blue police-officer costume. Nodding toward the cap hooked over the back of Luke's chair, he said, "Cool hat."

Luke yanked it from the spindle and placed it on his head, then bent sideways in his chair to eye the holster around Gabe's hips. "I asked for a gun an' hoe-ster, but Mommy said no way."

Josie was still silent, focusing on a single purple lollipop that hadn't been sorted into a pile.

"I know where to find a tool belt in your size," Gabe told Luke. "A hard hat, too. Maybe next year you could be a building contractor like me."

After extracting a piece of gum and a roll of hard candy from his pumpkin, Luke placed them carefully on the table before shaking his head. "No. I wanna be a pleece-man, like Daddy."

"I understand," Gabe said.

And he did. Josie's nephew hadn't met his father until he was a year old, but since then both Ethan and Luke had been making up for lost time. "Oh, well," Gabe said, shooting a teasing smirk toward Josie. "Maybe I can talk your aunt into being a contractor next year. She'd be less spooky in a tool belt than she is in a mustache, I think." He winked at Luke, who giggled.

Josie didn't respond at all. She sat clutching her paper sack and eyeing that damn lollipop, appearing very much as if she hadn't heard.

She was sure acting strange.

When Callie returned to the kitchen, Gabe and Josie said their goodbyes and returned to the car just as five gruesome-looking revelers passed the dark house.

Gabe watched Josie set the paper sack on her lap again. He'd thought it was a gift for her sister or the kids, but she'd carried it inside and back out again.

Josie didn't talk in the car, which left Gabe to wonder what could be so wrong. Callie was Lilly's mother, and she'd obviously decided to maintain as much normalcy as possible.

Gabe wondered how long it would take Josie to unload this new burden, whatever it was. "Something happen at Callie's that I missed?" he asked.

"Not that I know of."

More silence.

"Things okay at your work site this week?" he asked as they traveled through downtown Wichita. "Trouble with suppliers?"

She shifted in her seat, and Gabe prayed she'd snap out of it now. "Peter's pushing for me to finish the first model home by Thanksgiving," she said. And stopped talking.

Peter Kramer was a Wichita developer who had hired both of them for his current project. He was demanding, but fair. Gabe glanced across at Josie. "Gonna make it?"

She stared straight ahead. "Sure. I'm ordering draperies this week, and I scheduled the furniture to be delivered a week early."

Josie's tone was confident. She'd make a lot of money from this job, and she'd probably score a referral or two. Apparently, work wasn't the problem.

"Ethan and Callie have got a handle on this thing with Lilly," he said. "They'll work diligently to find answers. Lucky thing your sister does medical research for a living."

"Mm-hmm."

Okay. Josie didn't sound overly upset about Lilly. Not right now. But she acted…bothered. By *something*.

"And how's Isabel? Still enjoying Colorado life?"

"She loves it."

Gabe asked a few more questions about Josie's sisters, but she simply answered and didn't get enthused about her tales. And as soon as he stopped asking, she stopped talking. "What's bugging you, then, kid?"

"Nothing."

"You're completely distracted."

"No, I'm not."

"You hardly paid attention to Luke."

"Yes, I did. He commented on all our costumes. He thought it was strange that I was dressed as a guy."

"Oh, yeah? What did he want that he didn't have?"

"A gun and holster. He's asked for them every year since he was two. Callie always refuses."

"What did he say when I offered him a tool belt and hard hat?" Gabe asked.

"You didn't."

He caught her gaze, held it.

Josie sniffed. "I guess I missed that. I was probably watching Lilly."

"Callie had taken her out of the room by then."

Josie scowled.

"See? You're acting funny."

"If I am, it's none of your business."

He dropped the subject. In his family, everything was everyone's business. But Josie had grown up with a mother who'd held a high regard for privacy. This wasn't the first time Josie had told him to mind his own business. Perhaps she'd talk after they'd relaxed at the party for a while.

Or maybe Gabe would stop worrying about it. He'd decided he ought to start dating again—it'd been almost nine months since he'd had that fling with Kendra.

Gabe's married sister, Nadine, had said she might bring a single teacher friend tonight. She thought the woman and Gabe might hit it off.

Maybe Gabe would focus on his own good time. And Josie could talk when she was ready.

Chapter Four

Minutes later, Gabe neared his mom and stepdad's huge house just outside Wichita's northern city limits. Cars and trucks were already lined up along the grassy area between the house and barn. Gabe had to park next to the ditch, about fifty yards away.

As Josie started to get out of the car, she gaped at the bag in her hand. "Crud! I meant to give this to Luke."

"What is it?"

"Some of those cereal treats. I made them to resemble pumpkins and ghosts. He loves them."

Gabe wasn't surprised at the contents of the bag. Josie wasn't a cook, but she doted on her nephew. "Don't worry about it. He hauled in enough sugar to last him a while."

"Guess so." Josie left the bag in her seat and they began the long trek to the barn. The ground beneath them was uneven, so Gabe took Josie's elbow. Usually, they would have talked. Josie was still quiet, and that was strange, but Gabe wasn't supposed to let that bug him.

Gabe's mother had outdone herself with decorations. One side of the barn's double doors had been strung with cobwebs and spiders, and it appeared as if a life-sized witch had flown through the top front wall. Six torches lit the area just enough to show a black, bulbous backside, some broom bristles and a pair of boot-clad feet, all poking out of a painted, jagged hole. After Gabe had followed Josie into the barn quaking with spooky music, he spied the witch's green warted face and broken broom handle jutting through the other side.

Holding a diaphanous pink mermaid tail draped over an elbow, Cindy Connolley, Gabe's graying but ever-gorgeous mother, swished over to greet him and Josie and direct them to the drinks. "That's hot buttered rum in the cauldron," she said. Then she nodded toward a shaggy student type standing behind the table. "Otherwise, The Thing there will set you up."

"Thanks, Cindy." Josie immediately approached the young guy, then stood talking to him for a moment after he'd handed her a bottle of beer.

The Thing might be the hired help tonight, but he'd dressed for the party. With three surplus eyeballs dotting his forehead and four muscular arms—two held fake martinis—he should be able to handle the job.

Gabe was relieved to see Josie smiling. She leaned forward to peer at one of the guy's extra arms, then laughed about something he'd said.

If Josie's ailment was loneliness, this guy could be her cure. Apparently, he was a seasoned partyer.

He was a little *too* young, though. And scruffy. All five of his eyes ogled Josie's chest as he made some comment. Gabe could hazard a guess about what the other guy was saying.

The little runt had better be nice to Josie.

Turning toward his mother, Gabe muttered, "Who's he?"

"The Thing? Accountant in Kurt's business office. Graduated cum laude from Wichita State's business school."

"When—last week?"

"Maybe five, six years ago? He's probably close to thirty, Gabriel."

"He's okay? Nice to his mom? Avoids drugs and orgies?"

Furrows formed on his mother's brow. "I think so. You never know, really." She looked horrified for a moment before her expression cleared. "Oh, no. I remember meeting his parents once. He's fine."

As if a meeting of parents meant anything. Serial killers had parents, didn't they? "Hope so." Gabe forced his attention to the party decorations. "I love the crashed witch. You get the details right, don't you?"

"Guess you got that from me," she said, examining his mustache. "Is that real?"

Gabe had seen his mom a few days ago for dinner. Did women not realize that a decent mustache took weeks to grow? "Nope," he said. "Mine's as fake as Josie's."

Those twin lines creased his mother's face again. "You two haven't broken your 'just friends' pact, have you?"

"No. Why?"

"You're acting a bit odd, son. Sort of…overprotective. And you two did come dressed as a couple."

Gabe scanned the crowd, noting that Josie had left The Thing and was headed toward the dance area. "We're both dressed as men, Mom. Men who I presume were straight. And I only watch over Josie because she doesn't have anyone else to tackle the chore."

"Oh, okay, then," his mother said. "Well, the best costumed couple takes home the trophy, same as every year. Vote at the box near the snacks. Maybe you can woo the crowd and win."

"Yeah, right. Where's Kurt?" Gabe scanned the room.

"That fisherman dancing with one of the sexy bunnies."

Gabe followed his mother's pointed finger and spotted her husband. Slightly stouter and a decade older than Gabe's mother, Kurt Connolley had lost his hair ages ago. He nose was huge. He wasn't handsome, especially when compared with Gabe's late dad, but his mother so obviously loved her second husband. She always said she'd been lucky twice.

Kurt's costume was pretty standard—hip waders, multipocketed vest and floppy hat. However, the fishing pole he carried had a humongous hook, covered with sea-green glitter and baited with a pair of fluffy pink bedroom slippers.

To catch a mermaid.

Gabe laughed. "Nope. You'll keep another trophy."

His mother glided away to greet some new arrivals behind him, and Gabe noticed that Josie had perched herself cross-legged on a hay bale. She sipped from her bottle and watched the dancing couples.

Very un-Josie-like behavior.

Gabe followed her and plopped down one bale over. "You're not mingling?"

"No." She sighed.

"Want to talk about it?"

"No."

"Want to dance?"

"No."

He nodded, but remained near her for a moment longer in case she decided it was time to blab out her woes.

"Make your rounds," Josie said after another long, loud sigh. "I'll join you once I finish my drink."

Having two sisters and a mom, Gabe was very aware that "leave me alone" was often a veiled request for extra attention.

Josie generally said what she meant, though. He'd back off and let her brood awhile.

"I'll check back in a bit," he promised.

He returned to the bar for a soft drink before making his way through the crowd to greet his colleagues and survey the costumes. Josie wasn't ready to budge a half hour later, so he approached the dance area and was immediately snagged by a Minnie whose Mickey didn't dance. He danced one song with her, then another with the famous Kansas Dorothy.

Dorothy was otherwise known as Alana Morgan, one of his mother's Augusta acquaintances from way back. She and Cindy Connolley had worked together on the theater's planning board for a few years, and they still played cards on occasion.

After his waltz with Alana, Gabe's sisters arrived

to drag him away from the dance floor. Once more, Nadine and Livy had dressed as a pair—of salt and pepper shakers this year. Even with molded tinfoil hats and plastic-enclosed bodies, they were stunning. Blond and blue-eyed, like Gabe and his parents.

"You didn't bring anyone?" Gabe asked Nadine.

"Just me," Livy answered. "Frank stayed home with the kiddoes."

The twins practically spoke as one when they were together. Gabe rarely noticed.

"You know he hates crowds," Nadine explained.

Gabe had meant Nadine's teacher friend, not her husband. It didn't really matter, though. With Josie in a deep funk, he'd probably feel guilty if he danced the night away with a potential new girlfriend.

As he danced one song with each sister, Gabe watched Josie get up to nab another drink and talk to a couple of people. But she was still spending most of her time warming that bale of hay.

Josie had always been energetic. Easygoing. Even when she was upset about something, she carried on her normal activities and tried to ignore the problem.

But she didn't *mope*.

Gabe attacked her from behind, simultaneously grabbing an elbow and the hand holding her drink. He managed to haul her off the hay bale without splashing either of them with beer.

"What are you doing?" she demanded.

"Taking you to Mom's terrace."

"Why?"

"To talk."

"Don't need to." They passed a werewolf, a scrawny Arnold Schwarzenegger and the impaled witch.

"Going to." Gabe released Josie's hand outside the barn but kept hold of her elbow until they were rounding the corner to the terrace. After nudging her onto a cushioned lounge chair, he sat at its foot and studied her face under the glow of some ghost string lights.

She'd pulled off her mustache sometime between their arrival and now. With her hair slicked away from her face, she appeared young. Even in the faint light, those big hazel eyes registered melancholy.

She looked different. Older, maybe. Surely less bubbly and fun.

Infinitely more vulnerable.

Some Halloween magic must be in the air tonight. Happy souls had twisted into mournful ones and convivial feelings had slid toward the erotic.

Gabe wanted to pull Josie into his arms, kiss her, then whisper her worries away.

Instead, he got up to locate the switch near the back door. He flipped it to add more light to the terrace and scare away those thoughts.

Returning to the end of the chaise lounge, he sat down far enough from Josie to maintain a distance he'd appreciate tomorrow, but close enough that she'd have to force him off the chair to escape.

"Come on, kid. Spill."

Josie blinked at Gabe. "What?"

"You left your sister's house without giving your nephew his bag of treats, and now you're sitting around on a hay bale when you could be schmoozing. What's going on?"

She wasn't prepared to talk about her visit to Woodbine. Especially not to take-charge Gabe. First, he'd be perturbed that she'd snuck out without him. Then he'd tell her how she should have handled things.

That'd make her feel worse. So why bother?

Drinking a beer and a quarter without moving around must have affected Josie, or perhaps she needed an ear more than she'd realized, because she blurted out, "I met my father this weekend."

Gabe stared at her. "You... Already? Where is he?"

"Up in Woodbine." She chuckled, but her throat was tight and the sound came out rough.

Gabe settled a hand on her ankle. "Where is that, Josie? I've never heard of it. Is it in Kansas?"

"It's near Abilene." Josie held his gaze. He'd have to guide this conversation, because she sure couldn't. In a house full of women who'd ranted and talked and cried out their pain, Josie had been content to escape hers. She ate some chocolate or repaired the faucet drip or shot a game of pool with a buddy.

Why this compulsion to tell Gabe her stupid, insecure thoughts? She told him a lot, but not everything. Not her deepest worries. Heck, she was a party girl. She rarely had any deepest worries.

"What happened to upset you so much?"

Josie couldn't shake her disappointment, or her feeling that she'd opened Pandora's box. She took a long swallow of beer to dislodge the lump and send it on down her throat. "He didn't know me," she said.

"You must have introduced yourself."

She snorted. "I chickened out. I gave a fake name and implied that I was friends with the family. He asked about my sisters. He didn't mention a third child at all."

Gabe swore under his breath.

Josie was satisfied to see that he'd understood the strength of her reaction. He would. According to all reports, *his* dad had been wonderful—loving, open, affectionate. Too bad he'd died so young.

Gabe scooted closer and moved his hand from her ankle to her thigh. Rubbing. Soothing.

He'd done exactly that a hundred times before. Josie understood that he meant it in a friendly way. He couldn't know the thoughts he provoked in her.

"What did your sisters say about the meeting?" he asked. "And did you find out if your father has a history of seizures?"

"I haven't told my sisters yet. And I didn't ask about the seizures."

Gabe gave her a dark look.

"He said something about enjoying good health most of his life, though," she added.

When Gabe continued to glower at her, she let out an aggravated sigh. "I just went up there on Friday, and it was strange and hard. I've barely had time to process my thoughts about the experience."

"Is he okay?"

She sipped her drink, avoiding Gabe's steady gaze as she remembered her impressions of Rick Blume. "He's an old man," she said. "Tall. Quiet. Callie and

Isabel both have some of his features." She lifted her shoulders. "I don't. But the main thing that bothered me, really, was that he didn't acknowledge my existence."

Gabe took her drink and set it down on the terrace floor, then tugged her legs to the side of the chair so he could move closer. When he wrapped his arms around her, a couple of tears escaped and trickled down Josie's cheeks. She wiped them away with the back of her hand. "It was tough to talk about my sisters and leave myself out," she said against Gabe's warm chest. "He was so proud to hear about them."

"Plenty of people are proud of you, Josie. You don't need the approval of some stranger."

Josie felt Gabe's hand caress the back of her hair, then slip past her shoulder blades and down, until it rested at the curve of her waist.

His hand felt good there.

Too good.

She disentangled herself from the hug and reclined against the seat back. "I live alone in the same house where I grew up. I frequent the same places. Eat from the same cereal bowl every morning. What have I done with my life?"

I'm not special.

She didn't say it; she wouldn't risk tearing up again when Gabe would see. But she thought it.

"Is this what's eating at you?" Gabe asked. "That you went to meet this man who'd never bothered to send you a damn birthday card, and you didn't have more to show for yourself?"

Gabe was merely pointing out the error in her logic, but he'd also described the deepest source of an emotional trauma that didn't have to make sense to hurt.

"As I was telling him about my sisters, I realized something. The more I talked about them, the harder it became to reveal my identity to him."

"Why?"

She chuckled sadly. "Callie researches cancer and is married to a police helicopter pilot. She has two kids, both adorable, even if Lilly's health is a concern. And Isabel goes on dang mountain hikes every weekend with a handsome, intelligent husband and cherubic toddler."

"Mmm-hmm. You should be proud of them."

"I am. God, do I sound like a ninny or what? I feel like a three-year-old, crying because my sisters got something I didn't. Something I didn't really want in the first place."

"You're upset."

She nodded.

"Describe yourself now, Josie."

Hurt. Cold. Tired. In need of another serious hug and wishing I could get over this experience.

"Party girl," she said. "Likes sports and beer. Selfish, sometimes. Avoids love." She stopped herself before she said too much.

"You're anything but selfish," Gabe said. "And you avoid romantic intimacy, not love."

"Maybe."

"You're also an award-winning interior designer who volunteers time to charities. You're highly respected in the industry, especially for your children's rooms. Peter Kramer told me he's been very happy with your work."

"He's paying me very well for my work."

Gabe lifted his brows. "And that's a negative, how?"

Josie sipped her beer and stared out beyond the patio. "In my family, money was considered almost as evil as men."

He rolled his eyes. "Your mom might have taught you that, but she had problems."

Josie shrugged.

"Are you finished with this father quest?" Gabe asked.

"Nope. I intend to ask about his health history," she said, catching the censure in Gabe's gaze. "The question never fit. And after I realized Rick didn't know me, I couldn't think about anything else."

"Maybe you should just call him and ask," Gabe said. "I'd do that for you, if you like."

"You would?"

"Of course. And if you decide to go back to Woodbine, I could go with you. I could offer you my impressions of the man."

"You'd be willing to meet him?"

"Why not?"

"You'd have to sit and listen and not offer a speck of advice," Josie said, giving him a stern look. "This is my decision, and I have to do it my own way."

Gabe's jaw worked.

She was goading him, but it was important that she maintain control. "You'd be there for moral support. That's all."

"I heard you."

She'd have to think about it. If she did visit her father again, it'd be great to have a friend along. But a quiet friend, who was there to add to her confidence and not to her conflict. Gabe was prone to do both. And he was anything but quiet when it came to offering advice.

One thing was certain: she wasn't making this decision tonight, when she was supposed to be forgetting her troubles.

"I'm better now," she said, shoving at Gabe's chest to get him to move off the chair. "Let's head back to the party."

He leaned down to pick up her bottle, then stood. "I don't see why you didn't let me go with you last weekend."

"Your mother had you and your sisters over for an early dinner on Saturday, remember?" Josie got up and pulled her fake mustache from her pants pocket. "Didn't Nadine bring some teacher friend she thought you'd like?"

"No. The teacher friend couldn't make it on Saturday. She caught some virus going around her classroom. She was supposed to come to tonight's party, too. Guess she was still sick."

Josie restuck her mustache to the skin above her upper lip. "What? You haven't learned the teacher friend's name?" she teased.

"Miss Roberts," Gabe said, pleased with himself.

"No *first* name?"

He sighed dramatically as he handed Josie her bottle. "Nadine's kids have all had Miss Roberts for reading," he said. "I must have heard her last name a hundred times at Mom's dinner. Apparently, she's popular with the under-ten set."

At Josie's continued smirk, he said, "I wrote her first name down on the back of a piece of paper, along with her phone number. I'm supposed to call her."

"Another scrap for the dryer's lint trap?"

"No. I *asked* for her number, and I told Nadine to give her mine. I intend to…" Gabe faltered, then he stepped nearer to Josie.

He was close enough that she could see the markings of his eyes, even in the dim light.

She could feel his breath, warm on her face.

What would it feel like to kiss Gabe? She'd wondereed often enough. Why did she get the feeling that one kiss from Gabe would knock all thoughts of anything else clear out of her head?

But Gabe cupped her chin with one hand and pursed his lips, then studied hers as he unstuck one side of her mustache and adjusted it.

Good heavens! He was fixing her costume—surely a brotherly gesture. Five years ago, Josie would've considered it so. Heck, five days ago she would have been certain of it.

Tonight she wished for more from Gabe than his brotherly affection, more than his platonic touch. She wished he'd hold her the way a man holds a desirable woman.

She chided herself. She should be glad Gabe wasn't thinking along the same line she was. At least one of them was sane.

When Gabe finished her mustache adjustment, his finger grazed her bottom lip. Then, as if he'd left a bright scarlet mark there, his eyes traced the path of his finger.

Josie wasn't smirking now, and neither was Gabe. They were standing close. Staring at each other.

Josie didn't know what Gabe was thinking, but some crazy part of her willed him to lean down a few inches and drag his lips across that same burning spot.

That would help her forget her father's neglect. It would also erase any positive thoughts about a popular reading teacher right out of Gabe's head, at least temporarily.

It'd be a mistake.

In-control Gabe wouldn't forget all the reasons they shouldn't cross that line.

He didn't kiss her, of course. He dropped his hands, blinked those baby blues, then stepped away from her. "Ready to head back?" he asked.

"Sure."

They trudged through the darkness, both quiet. Josie felt she should hold her breath as she waited for the moment one of them finally did or said something normal.

Would they joke about the moment between them on the patio, or ignore it? What if she said something about it and discovered that he really didn't feel anything? That he'd been thinking about Miss Roberts or clearing some stray mustache hair.

Could Josie handle another rejection so soon after that disastrous meeting with her father?

Gabe broke the silence just before they reached the barn. "What time should we leave on Saturday?"

Thank heaven, a run-of-the-mill question, and undoubtedly the best way to handle the situation. Josie expelled a loud breath.

Then she processed what he'd said.

"Wait a minute, *this* Saturday?"

"Sure."

Josie would not be bullied into inviting Gabe along. She'd never even decided whether she was going.

And now, Gabe was becoming more and more of a distraction. She was certain she needed to go alone.

When she went.

If she went.

"I'm not ready to go back this soon," she said as they reentered the barn doors to join a more relaxed and louder crowd. The stereo had been turned up to compete with the laughing and talking.

"You sure?" Gabe half shouted over the noise.

Usually, Josie loved being a single adult. She could attend a Halloween party on a work night, and not worry about babysitters or bedtimes.

Tonight she yearned for a curfew so she could leave now and avoid Gabe's query. "Won't you have a date with Miss Roberts this weekend?"

"Not if I don't make one," he said. "Besides, the visit with your dad would be in the daytime, wouldn't it? I could be home in plenty of time for a late date."

Ouch. She'd rather not hear about Gabe's plans with Miss Roberts. She'd simply been trying to change the subject.

Josie faced Gabe, making sure she had his full attention before shaking her head. "Don't push, Gabriel Thomas."

He extended her an elbow. "It's your call, Josie Blume."

"Good." She hooked a hand around his arm, and as they had numerous times in the past, they made their way through the crowd. They greeted colleagues, friends and rivals. Josie schmoozed until she was hoarse. When she found herself at the edge of the dance floor with Gabe, it felt natural to step into the crush of strangely dressed couples with him, so she did.

They'd danced together before. When neither of them was dating, they went out together all the time. She knew which songs he preferred, and she considered him an accomplished two-step partner.

And yet, tonight felt different.

Gabe's hands against her back were as proper as they'd ever been, but she admitted she'd been aching for them to touch her. She coveted the warmth of Gabe's embrace and the comfort of his voice.

What had changed?

She had. Josie herself. She felt unsteady, vulnerable…fragile. She needed a set of sturdy shoulders to lean on right now, and Gabe's were as broad as anyone's.

She needed his friendship. His strength.

That was all this was.

Wasn't it?

Chapter Five

With a quilt wrapped around her shoulders, Josie stepped onto the welcome mat on her front porch and surveyed the lawn, looking for the *Gazette*. One of the benefits of living in her mother's old house was that her closest neighbors were a quarter mile away. She could prance around out here buck naked, and no one would see.

Dang it. The paper was under the sweet gum tree, way out near the edge of the yard. That new carrier wasn't even getting it close. Next time she saw her, Josie would invite the girl over and teach her how to throw accurately from car window to porch.

Josie stepped off the porch and felt an icy crunch beneath her bare feet. Hard to believe it was this late in the year already. This afternoon, she'd drain the garden hoses and store them in the shed. Maybe she'd also gather menu ideas for Thanksgiving dinner. She'd phone Isabel and Callie to find out what they meant to contribute, then tell them about her meeting with their father.

But only if she found the courage to tell Rick who she was, in a little while. She intended to drink her coffee while she scanned the headlines, and then get moving.

As Josie traipsed across the lawn, crisp grass blades broke beneath her feet and stung so much she finished the trip on her toes. She should try to locate her scuffs. Maybe they were under the bed.

Just after she'd bent down to retrieve the paper, she heard a car approach. Standing quickly, she gathered the blanket tighter at her chest and watched Gabe pull into the drive behind her truck. Hadn't she told him she was busy this morning?

She was sure she had. She wanted to show up on her father's doorstep again, sit down in that awful floral chair and start fresh. She'd envisioned the whole scenario. She'd tell her father that there had been a third child—*her*—and ask if he'd known that her mother was pregnant again.

This visit was no whim. Josie had even called Brenda to set up a time. However, she hadn't planned to tell Gabe about it until after her return. Even if he sat there with his trap shut, he'd likely look at her in some certain way and make her lose track of her intentions.

Since the night of the party, Gabe had been big and ever-present in her thoughts. He'd surely be too big and present in the small front room of her father's Woodbine house.

Josie aimed a scowl toward Gabe's car window, then bounded up the front steps and went inside to wait.

He followed her in within seconds. "What were you doing outside in this weather, dressed like that?" He stood in her doorway, pointing at her bare legs.

She glanced down at the red pinwheel quilt Isabel had given her for Christmas last year. The blanket material was thick, and it covered her from chest to knees. Gabe couldn't know what she had on, or didn't, underneath. "I'm covered," she said. "What are you doing here this early?"

"Checking on you. Heading out of town today?"

She lifted her chin. "Why would you think that?"

"Mom told me you'd been asked to help with the Habitat house over in Douglass this morning, and you claimed you were busy."

"I am."

"Doing what? You told *me* you were too busy to catch the game. I assumed you were helping with the Habitat house."

"I don't tell you everything I do."

He eyed the top of the quilt material, then lifted his gaze to hers. "If you're headed to Woodbine, you know I'm willing to go."

"I know." Josie watched Gabe's eyes drift to her nearly bare shoulder again.

And stick.

She wore panties and a tank top to bed. In the summertime, she slept nude. She couldn't remember where she'd left her robe, and Gabe had seen her in less clothing plenty of times.

That *moment* the other night had done a number on her. She'd faltered. Allowed her simmering feelings to bubble over. She was more aware of Gabe. More aware that at any time, he could be thinking about her in the same way she was thinking about him.

Wishing he was.

And at the same time, hoping all this oddness would die down quickly.

Now she felt naked in front of him. She imagined that his expression held a heightened caring, his eyes a new heat. Her body responded to the idea. Her nipples tingled. Her thighs loosened.

She thought of sex. Hot, fast, toe-warming, worry-busting sex.

She yanked the quilt toward her chin.

Gabe's eyes darkened, then he turned to move an edge of the drapes to peer out the window.

God. She still wasn't feeling normal. Maybe today's visit with her father would help.

Today's visit with her father, *alone*.

"It's nice of you to offer to go, Gabe, but—"

"But what?" He faced her again.

"But I don't want anyone with me."

"Why not? I could go along for the ride. I wouldn't interfere."

Gabe meant what he was saying; she could tell. "You'd keep your mouth shut?"

"Of course."

"And if I get halfway there and decide to turn around again?" She'd done exactly that last Saturday. She'd come home to find Gabe watching the game in her living room. They'd traded keys several years ago. He safeguarded her place when she was away, and she did the same for him.

Maybe the key trade was a bad idea now.

Gabe held her gaze. "You do what you have to do, Josie. I'd only go to support you. I swear."

"What if I make it to Woodbine, but chicken out on his porch step?"

Gabe stepped closer, then bent his knees so he and Josie were eye-to-eye. "I. Won't. Say. A. Word."

She regathered the quilt into a fist at her neck. "Good. Then I'll go get dressed."

"Good. I'll wait." His voice carried the same tone it might have if he'd said, *Good. I won.*

The dang show-off.

After hurling her flaming body down the hall to her bedroom, Josie pulled clothes from her dresser drawers and started for the hallway bathroom. Even while she closed the door behind herself, she thought of something. She reopened the door to holler out, "Gabe?"

"Yes, Josie?"

"You might want to move your car. I'm driving."

"The beemer has cruise control."

"The truck's gas pedal works just fine."

"The car has a great stereo system."

She hadn't had time to react to that statement before he added. "And I bought the new Maroon Five CD."

"You did? Oh, wow. I *lovvve* their new song." Josie waited three beats and added, "But we're still taking the truck."

She giggled as she closed the door again, comfortable with their old, familiar banter. Gabe didn't even like Maroon Five all that much. He must have bought the CD as a lure. Maybe he was curious about her father. Perhaps that was why he was here all the time these days.

Her prealarm dream that had him showing up at her

bedside to confess that he'd developed the hots for her was just another crazy notion.

She'd liked the dream, though.

She'd hit the snooze bar twice, dozing longer to entertain the idea in that illogical state between dreams and waking.

Now that she was fully awake, the thought could be moved right back into the crazy category. Or the too-many-reasons-why-not category, at least.

She'd talk him out of the CD later.

She was just turning on the taps, when she heard her front door slam. Gabe must have gone out to move his car. She found herself grinning again.

Forty minutes later, she sat behind her steering wheel, flying up the highway toward Woodbine while Gabe fiddled with the radio dial. After about two songs, however, he clicked the radio off again. "Does your father know who you are yet?" he asked.

"No."

"Why'd you say you were coming?"

"I claimed that I wanted to bring pictures of his grandkids. Brenda said he'd be home all day. She said he'd be excited."

"He should be." Gabe stared out the window. After a moment, he asked, "Your father didn't sound forgetful or confused that first trip?"

"He was pretty sharp, I think."

Gabe didn't ask anything else. After they'd passed the turn for Marion Lake, he started talking about a bid he was compiling to do an extensive office remodel for a Wichita bread supplier. Josie's questions carried them all the way to Rick and Brenda's bumpy driveway.

Her father was outside today, wearing a huge blue parka and puttering near the chain-link pens.

"That him?" Gabe asked quietly as she parked behind the bigger pickup.

"Yep."

"You were right. Your sisters do have his build."

Josie eyed the older man. "Makes me wonder where *I* came from." When she noticed Gabe's startled look, she added, "Just joking. But I am worried about a lot of things today. Mostly about how he'll react to the news."

"He'll be fine."

Remembering her father's dependence on pills, Josie studied the frail-looking older man. Rick Blume seemed so nice. Nothing at all like what she'd expected based on her mother's descriptions. She liked him, she thought.

Whatever happened, she didn't want to hurt him. "I changed my mind," she told Gabe. "I do need your input. If you think I should shut up, jab me in the ribs or something, okay?"

"Why would you need to shut up?"

"If I start talking too much or not enough or…well, anything. I'm completely nervous."

"You don't get completely nervous."

"I do now. So help me?"

"That's why I'm here."

She might have coached Gabe more, but her father was already nearing the truck in big, welcoming strides.

After retrieving her billfold from the glove compartment, Josie hopped out. "Hi, there," she said. "I hope you don't mind that I brought a friend. This is Gabe Thomas."

Her father shook Gabe's hand. "Thomas?" he queried, glancing between the two of them. "She's a Thomas. Am I to assume that you are this young lady's husband? Her brother?"

Crud. Once again, Josie had forgotten about the fake name. "Uh, he's my husband," she said.

Gabe's eyebrows shot up.

She'd asked him to pose as her boyfriend plenty of times, but never as her husband. And she could just as easily have said he was her brother. But *husband* was the word that had popped out of her mouth, so for the few moments between now and her confession, she'd be Gabe's pretend wife. No big deal.

As they headed inside, Rick Blume told them that Brenda had taken all the dogs to a veterinarian's office in nearby Abilene for their annual shots. He hung his coat and Gabe's jacket on a rack near the front door, but Josie kept her sweater on. She was still cold. The truck's heater needed some work.

"Is Brenda your wife?" Gabe asked on their way to the living room, causing Josie to find *his* rib with *her* elbow.

"I'm in charge," she mouthed. "Not you."

Gabe lifted his shoulders.

"She might as well be my wife," Rick said, unaware of the drama going on behind his back. "We've been together for over twenty-five years."

Josie nodded, feeling awkward, and then drew the picture sleeve from her billfold. There was another moment of confusion when Gabe sat down on the tea-towel end of the sofa, but her father simply claimed the chair, then Josie took a seat next to Gabe.

She handed the pictures across to her father and started listing the children's names and ages.

No matter how loudly her mind shouted it, she couldn't bring herself to say that she was the children's doting aunt and *his* third child.

After Rick had chuckled over every picture and listened to a few cute kid stories, Josie folded the photos into her wallet, then watched Gabe pull the towel from beneath his thigh.

"You care for some coffee?" her father asked, standing.

"No," Josie said, surprising herself with a burst of bravery. "And I'm not married to Gabe. We're friends. He's here to support me today."

Rick lowered himself into the chair again and leveled a questioning gaze her way.

"My name's Josie—Josephine Sarah Blume." She studied her father, watching as his expression progressed through several degrees of agitation.

Finally, he shook his head. "You gave a false name before?"

He'd heard her real name, hadn't he? *Josie Blume?* Of course she'd given a false name. She was the daughter he'd never bothered to meet. How many people would feel courage when sitting in front of the person who'd caused such insult to their lives?

Josie glanced at Gabe, then took a deep breath and said, "I'm Callie and Isabel's little sister, Rick. I'm Ella's third daughter."

His expression grew more confused, and Josie actually felt sorry for him. "You are?" he asked.

"I was born on October twelfth, twenty-seven years ago."

"I see." He didn't look as though he did.

"Didn't you know about me?"

He took off his glasses and wiped them on his pants, then replaced them on his face and peered at her with an odd expression. Pain? Regret? Finally, he stared down at his knees.

He was wearing the same blue shirt and tattered pants that he'd worn two weeks ago. Today, Josie noticed that the toe of his left shoe had lifted from its sole. He looked tired. Old.

Josie didn't mean to make this overly hard on him. She felt they could take their time getting to know each other. She could be gracious. She'd simply wanted him to know who she was.

Maybe she should leave now. She could let the knowledge of her identity sink in, and come back another time to ask about Lilly and pursue whatever connection they could find.

"I couldn't have been sure that Elly was pregnant, but I suppose I'm not shocked," her father said. Then he sat up in the chair and added more forcefully, "If I'd have been aware of your identity two weeks ago, I might have said something."

"Right, well. I didn't tell you then."

He kept his gaze low. What was the man's fascination with his own knees?

"I'm telling you now."

"Right, well," her father echoed.

The moment was absurdly clumsy. Josie felt as though she'd stepped into a long, dark tunnel this morning, and had just made it through to the other side. But she wasn't sure yet which planet she was currently on.

Though she understood so much more now, new questions popped up every time Rick Blume answered one. Her father was obviously upset and confused, she was sure as heck upset and confused and she had no clue about what to say or do next.

Gabe shifted closer, and the new slant of the sofa cushion caused her body to tilt in his direction. She allowed herself to rest against his comforting solidness.

She turned toward him, sending a silent appeal, then smiled softly when he gave a slight nod.

He could help her through this.

He *intended* to help her through this. Thank heaven.

GABE MOVED HIS HAND over Josie's palm and squeezed gently, then let go. "Josie wanted to meet you for a specific reason," he told Rick Blume. "She didn't show up here to give you a hard time about leaving the family all those years ago."

Rick lifted his eyes to Gabe's. "All right."

"She has questions about any health problems. One of her sister's kids—Callie's baby daughter, Lilly—has had a couple of seizures in the past two months."

The old man sat forward in the chair, his expression intent. "Seizures? Is she okay?"

"We aren't certain. The first might have been related to a fever, but the second wasn't. She's also showing other mild signs of a neurological disorder."

"That's awful." Rick blinked those watery gray eyes. "I'm very sorry."

"We all are," Josie said. "But thanks."

Rick nodded, moving the briefest glance to Josie before staring at his knees again.

"Josie's wondering if you have any family history of seizure disorders," Gabe continued. "Or if not you, then your parents or anyone further back."

"I don't believe so," Rick said. "My parents lived long, healthy lives. I never heard of my grandparents having that kind of health problems, either. I can try to find out."

"I'd appreciate it." Josie stared at the old guy, but he still avoided her gaze. She leaned forward. "I'm not here only to get a health history, though," she said. "I have tons of questions about everything. I do want to understand why you left us. But I realize that this might be tough for you. I can return another time if you like."

Rick stood up. "I'm needing a drink. If you don't want coffee, how about some tea? Or something else. I'm not sure what Brenda has in there."

"Actually, that coffee sounds good about now," Gabe said at the same time that Josie said she'd drink some hot tea.

Rick went into the kitchen and soon returned with two steaming cups on saucers, then made another trip to bring out a glass of water. He gulped half of it, then sat down and rested the glass against his knee.

Finally, he looked at Gabe again. "A while before I left, Ella and I had stopped living as a married couple." He moved his gaze to Josie, but only for as long as it took to say those last two words.

Then he shook his head. "I felt I had to leave, but I was slow in going because I hated abandoning the girls. I wanted to find work first. Wanted Elly to keep our savings."

A lot of men in Rick's position might be inclined to list the various acts of selflessness prefacing their departure—especially if they struggled with guilt.

Hopefully, Josie would focus on the complexity of the situation rather than the failings of the man.

But Josie wouldn't be Josie if she wasn't direct. "Why would you think you had to leave the mother of your children?"

Rick's head dropped forward. Gabe thought he might have fainted, until he noticed that the man was glaring at his knees again.

The movement must have frightened Josie, who shot halfway out of her seat and sloshed tea onto her jeans. Catching hold of her waist, Gabe pulled her gently backward until she was relaxing against him. He took her cup and set it on the side table. Then he rubbed a hand against her lower back for a few moments, comforting her.

"Your mother thought I was weak," Rick muttered to Josie without meeting her eyes. "During those last weeks, she repeated the word *dimwit* so often I started to think that was exactly what I was—a dimwit. A dimwit to stay."

Josie nodded, her face chalky.

Ella Blume had vilified men in general and the girls' father specifically. Gabe had heard this via the Augusta grapevine and from all three of the Blume sisters.

Josie had often said that she wished her mother had lived to meet Gabe. That he would somehow prove the entire male population worthwhile.

For exactly that reason, he was sort of glad he hadn't met Ella. The burden was huge. In fact, Ella had met Ethan, Callie's husband and a great guy. She hadn't liked him.

"If you were aware of Mother's mental state, how could you leave Callie and Isabel with her?" Josie asked.

Rick didn't hesitate. "She was strong. Sharp-tongued. But she was so smart. I guess she convinced me she could raise any child better than I could."

He studied Gabe, then his knees, then the glass. He acted as if he was hiding something. Which made Gabe worry about what else Josie might learn today.

"Elly had some physical problems," Rick said. "Female problems. Even if she was pregnant, I couldn't have been certain that she'd carry the child. She lost a few babies early in the pregnancies. The muleheaded woman would never go to the doctor."

"She would never go later, either," Josie said. "My sisters and I suspected she was sick a few years back, but we never thought she'd have cancer. She lived so healthy."

"Guess you never know."

"Guess you don't."

Gabe decided to change the subject now, before Rick said anything else about the circumstances and timing of Josie's conception.

"Josie isn't the type to brag, but she's a remarkable woman," he said. "She works as an interior designer, and she's done children's rooms that have received national recognition."

Rick shot another glance at Josie. "You're creative, then."

"Guess so."

"Your mother was, too, of course." The old cuss finally looked at Josie for longer than a few seconds. "I probably am a dimwit. You had to spell things out to me."

"No. No, you're fine." Josie slid off the sofa and stepped forward to offer the old guy a hug.

A generous gesture that didn't surprise Gabe a bit. Sometimes he wondered how any of the Blume sisters managed to be so loving, given their childhood situation.

Rick Blume lifted halfway out of the chair and clutched his half-empty water glass in one hand as he patted Josie's back with the other.

"Thank you for seeing me today," she said. Then she turned to Gabe and gave him a look he'd seen hundreds of times before.

She was ready to go home. Now.

"We'd better get going," Gabe said, making a play at stretching before coming to his feet. "Josie and I both have a busy day ahead of us."

Rick set his glass on the coffee table and walked them to the door. As Gabe slipped into his coat, he decided that the old gossip might have been false after all.

Thank God.

Josie had only learned that Rick hadn't been aware of a third daughter. That he'd left when his wife's pregnancy was still in doubt. She was unaware of the other stories Gabe had heard.

If the rumors had been true, Rick would have explained his departure more thoroughly. What man wouldn't?

Gabe hoped Josie was satisfied with this meeting, despite her father's unenthusiastic response to her. She might not have discovered a loving father pining away for his lost children, but she'd received the health information she'd sought.

Maybe that would be enough.

But when Rick opened the front door, Josie started to walk through and then hesitated, turning to Rick again and ensnaring his gaze before he could avoid hers. "Isabel is coming to Kansas in a couple of weeks, and she's bringing her family for Thanksgiving. Would you like the chance to meet everyone?"

Rick stepped backward, bumping against the door and knocking it into the wall. The tired old face that had remained amazingly disimpassioned today had changed. Josie's suggestion had stunned the poor guy.

Gabe knew the feeling.

Josie wasn't finished with this? Hadn't she noticed that the man had barely looked at her this morning?

Rick stared at Josie now, his expression incredulous. Then he started hemming and hawing, saying something about Brenda and their plans, the dogs and the weather. His discomfort was so evident it made Gabe squirm.

"Think about it, okay?" Josie prompted. "You could visit on the Friday after the holiday. All of us girls would be there. All the kids, too. Of course Brenda's invited, also."

The old man's face relaxed, as if he could at least fathom the idea with his helpmate attached to it. "I'll talk to her about our plans for that day."

Josie nodded. "Good."

Before anyone could say anything else, Gabe ensnared Josie's hand and led her outside, down the steps and to her vehicle. He opened her truck door, waited until she got in, then went around to the passenger seat. As soon as he sat beside her, he put a thumb on her chin and nudged her face his direction. "Isabel's coming for Thanksgiving?" he asked.

"For that whole long weekend, yes."

He dropped his hand.

"Does she know you've talked to Rick Blume?"

"Not yet."

"Callie, neither, I suppose."

"No. Callie, neither." Josie shifted in her seat, eyeing Rick and Brenda's modest house, then laughed heartily. With each chuckle, she seemed to expel a heartful of emotion. "My mother must be thrashing in her grave."

"I'd say so."

Josie turned her key in the ignition. "Go ahead, call me impulsive," she said as she circled out of the drive.

"You are that, kid."

"It'll be fine."

"I hope so."

Lord, did he hope so.

Chapter Six

"I'm getting stuffed. You want the rest of my burger?" Josie mumbled as she nibbled on one last French fry.

"No. I'm good." Gabe crumpled his sandwich wrapper and tossed it into the large paper sack, then picked up his soft drink and sipped as he leaned against a pillar of Josie's porch.

The drive from Woodbine had put them at Augusta's city limits at lunchtime, and Josie had insisted on buying the meal to repay Gabe for his support.

He'd done well, butting in only when necessary. And he'd allowed her to wallow in silence all the way home.

This visit with her father had been as upsetting as the first, though in a different way.

"I can't believe how much it's warmed up today." She stared out over a yard filled with sun-glistening yellow grass that didn't look as though it had been frozen this morning.

"November in Kansas."

Josie folded the wrapper around the remains of her

sandwich and put it in the sack along with the French fry bag. Then she finished her cola and set the cup down.

A squirrel scampered across a tree limb and she watched it, wishing life didn't feel so complicated right now.

Wishing her father had shown more remorse for his years of neglect. Wishing she'd felt that easy connection to him.

Josie wished things with Gabe could go back to easy, too. He couldn't know how much it had meant to her to feel his hand on hers today. To feel his touch on her back. How much his presence had bolstered her courage.

She was supposed to be gutsy all by herself.

"You finished?" Gabe asked as he gathered the sack and cups. "I'll take these to the trash."

He'd been so patient with her. Trying to cajole her to talk. Allowing her to be quiet when his efforts didn't work. Gabe understood her, maybe more than anyone.

Maybe more than she did herself.

He disappeared inside, and Josie leaned back on her arms and stretched out her legs.

This visit with her father had left her feeling more confused, rather than less. So much didn't add up. She could be obsessing. Putting more meaning into Rick's odd reaction to her than she should.

But she didn't think so.

As soon as Gabe had stepped outside again, she said to him, "Did you notice that Rick wouldn't even look at me this morning?"

Gabe sat beside her on the step and didn't comment. He simply faced her, waiting.

Oh, yeah. He knew her.

"He looked at you, not me," Josie said. "He acted almost as if he was…*afraid.* Of me! Can you imagine?" She laughed, but her attempt at breezy couldn't have fooled Gabe. She sounded disturbed.

And she had a right to be upset. Her father had just rejected her in yet another way. Her father, who gave the appearance of being some harmless old man.

Had both her parents been unbalanced? The thought wasn't encouraging. Josie already worried about becoming as set in her ways as Ella. Or an alcoholic like her father.

But Rick hadn't given the impression that he had a drinking problem, had he?

Another thing that didn't add up.

Gabe put his arm around her, tugging her close. "Aw hell, Josie. Who knows what Rick was thinking. Don't let his behavior get to you."

She leaned into Gabe's warmth. His strength. Still, she shivered from an overflow of emotion.

"Remember when I hugged him?" she asked. "Just before we left?"

"Mmm-hmm."

"His body felt so skinny and foreign. I like Rick, but…well, it's almost as if I'm having to dig to find some caring from him."

She leaned backward to see Gabe's expression, curious about his reaction.

His gorgeous blue eyes glowed bright with the

concern she'd craved from her father. She lowered her voice to a whisper. "I felt as though I was hugging someone else's dad."

Gabe pulled her into his embrace and held her for a long time. He felt solid and good. Familiar. Interested in her the way no one else was.

"These things take time, Josie," he murmured against her hair. "You'll get to know Rick better and vice versa."

"Especially since I opened my big mouth and invited him to a dang dinner I wasn't planning. Why do I forget that I don't cook big meals?"

"Do you want me to come to the dinner?"

She edged away. "Don't you usually work the day after Thanksgiving?"

"Usually," he said. "But I could—"

"No. I'll be fine," Josie interrupted. "I need to see him without you being there to save me. Maybe Rick…maybe *my father* and I will establish that missing connection if we don't have you around to smooth our awkwardness."

"Your sisters will be there."

"He needs to connect with them, too." Josie heard a ringing from inside. "That's my phone."

She got up and swung past the screen door, catching the kitchen phone on the third ring.

"Josie?"

It was Callie.

"Yes, Cal. Everything okay?"

"Where've you been?" Callie asked, her voice abnormally husky. "We've left messages, tried your cell phone. Ethan was going to find a computer so he could e-mail you."

Josie shoved this morning's newspaper off the answering machine and realized it was blinking a six. She'd had six messages, presumably from Callie and Ethan.

"Sorry, Cal. I went out with Gabe this morning. Guess I neglected to check the machine when we got home. What's up?"

"Lilly had a seizure this morning," Callie said. "Another bad one that lasted a half hour."

Josie leaned against her counter. "What happened?"

"I noticed her staring into space during her morning bath, and then she started convulsing. We took her to the E.R. right away."

Josie realized she was trembling. "Is she okay?"

"She's sleeping now, and we've consulted with the Kansas City neurologist over the phone. He said he'd give her more time on this medication, but up the dosage. They're keeping her at the hospital to run an EEG and some other tests."

"My God, Cal. This is awful."

"I know." Callie spoke in a low tone. Josie could tell she was very upset. "We'll see the new neurologist in his office the week after Thanksgiving."

"Good. Is Luke there with you?"

"No. We were going to have you watch him, but got hold of a neighbor first."

Josie cast a gaze around the kitchen, searching for her truck key. "I'll be right there."

"No. Don't come," Callie said. "The nurses probably

won't let you in the room, anyway. We're keeping Lilly very quiet."

"Then I'll go get Luke and wait at your house with him. He'll probably feel better at home."

"Hon, no. Leave Luke be. He's playing with the neighbor's kid—something he usually does on Saturday afternoon. If we have to stay overnight, I'll call you back."

"Should I telephone Isabel?" Josie asked.

"I've already talked to her twice."

Josie felt useless.

She could do one thing now, though. A very small thing. It was time to tell Callie about Rick. "I'm sorry about Lilly, Cal. And I have something to confess."

"What is it, Josie? I only have a minute or two."

"I went to see our dad."

"Josie, what?"

"Gabe went with me this morning. Rick Blume lives in Woodbine, north of here. And, well, I've been there once before." Josie heard the hospital intercom and recognized this wasn't the time for details. "Don't worry, it was okay. I'll tell you about it later. I just thought I'd tell you he doesn't have a seizure disorder, and he doesn't believe there's a family history of them."

"Thanks for finding out." Callie hesitated, then said, "I have to go, hon. Ethan's waving at me from the hallway. We're fine. We have each other."

Josie hung up, then pushed the answering machine's play button and listened to her sister and Ethan's messages, starting just a few minutes after she'd left with Gabe this morning.

Why was her life so troubled lately? Josie hated to think about Lilly, suffering. Hated to see Cal and Ethan go through such an awful time.

Hated too many unanswered questions.

She felt a presence behind her. Gabe.

"You okay, kid?" he asked.

She didn't turn around. "Callie telephoned about Lilly," she said, hearing the tremor in her own voice. "She had another seizure. Worse, I guess. They're at the hospital. They've been calling all morning."

She opened her cabinet, heaven knows why, and stared inside without seeing. "I feel so useless."

Gabe shut the cabinet door and pulled her against his chest, surrounding her with strong arms that felt so good.

So right.

The only right thing in her life at the moment.

He felt nothing like a brother.

"It'll be okay," he murmured against her hair. "I believe Lilly will be fine eventually. Callie and Ethan will move mountains to discover the cause of the seizures. They'll urge the doctors to move mountains."

"I hope they find out soon and get them stopped."

"I do, too. But whatever happens, with Lilly *or* with Rick Blume, you'll handle it."

"I hope so."

Gabe rotated her in his arms and tipped her face to his, offering a smile not as dazzling as usual but very real. Very Gabe. "You're a brave, strong woman, Josie Blume. You'll handle it." He kissed her temple.

She wanted so badly to connect to him in a deeper way. To stop denying what she craved from him.

What she'd needed from him for a long time.

She stood on tiptoe and caught his eyes, communicating her desire psychically.

If he'd had those feelings for her at all, he would recognize her invitation.

He cocked his head slightly. After noting her gaze, he let out a barely perceptible snort, then bent and touched his mouth to hers. But he held the kiss at a simple peck, like those he'd given her before.

Brotherly.

She moved forward for a second try. Instead of pursing her lips and smacking them quickly against his, as she usually did, she kept her mouth soft.

Showed him her need.

He backed away just a whisper, then held there, making her wonder a thousand things in that tenth of a second. Then, at last, he settled his lips over hers again.

He kissed her long. Tenderly, softly. Communicating returned desire even while maintaining an element of respect and caring.

His kiss wasn't too hot, but it was sweeter than anything she could imagine. It also revealed a truth that neither of them had ever dared voice.

They each wanted more.

NEARLY TWO WEEKS LATER, Josie stood at that same kitchen counter, loading the dishwasher while her family filled the room with their sounds and motions. Luke finished a slice of cherry pie at the table, while Izzy's sweetheart one-year-old, Darlene, sat at a high chair nibbling on a breadstick. In a second high chair, a calm but sleepy Lilly fingered a bowl of pumpkin puree.

Callie and Isabel flanked all three kids, discussing baby-food brands and recent baby firsts. Ethan and Trevor sat at the table with Rick, arguing over the calls in one of yesterday's televised bowl games.

They all made such an appearance of *normal*.

Josie was glad that Rick had decided to come, even without Brenda. He'd debated it, by his own admission, and had ultimately concluded that he couldn't resist the chance to meet his grandchildren.

And the day had gone well. Josie's lasagna had been a hit, the conversation had flowed and the kids had been delightful. The entire evening could be considered a complete success.

As Josie listened to the men's conversation, she made a few comments—after all, she was as much a sports fan as either of her brothers-in-law—but she spent more time trying to pinpoint the source of her agitation.

"How did you celebrate Thanksgiving when you were a child, Rick?" Callie asked during a moment of quiet. "Did you have big family dinners?"

"Not like yours," he said, turning to her. "I grew up on a farm, and we always had a turkey and fixins'. We never had other people there, though. Just me and my parents. And now it's mostly just me and Brenda."

"Sorry she couldn't make it today," Izzy said.

"I know. One of the dogs is ready to deliver. We always try to have some pups ready for Christmas."

"I'm sure that's a good idea."

Isabel sounded so cordial.

And that was it, wasn't it?

That was what was bothering Josie. Her sisters were so *polite,* treating Rick as though he was a distant uncle or respected acquaintance rather than the father that had gone missing over twenty-seven years ago.

Once again, she felt different and moody and confused. Why wasn't anyone asking questions? And why wasn't Rick trying harder to explain his absence from their lives?

Josie slammed a coffee cup into the top rack and hit another, causing a clank that had everyone else looking up. "Oops," she said in an overly sweet tone. "Wouldn't want to break such *nice* coffee cups."

She washed a handful of forks, dropped half on the floor and swore a little too loudly as she bent to pick them up.

"You okay, hon?" Callie asked.

Before she could answer, Luke popped out of his chair. "I'm done," he said. "Can I be skewzed?"

"*May* I be *ex*-cused," Callie corrected.

Luke repeated his mother's words using the same inflection. As soon as Callie said yes, Luke grabbed the toy tractor he'd received from Rick today. "*May* I go *out*-side?" he asked.

"Yes," Ethan said, grinning. "But wear your coat and stay in the yard."

Luke found his coat quickly, then submitted to Callie's buttoning before grabbing the tractor again. As soon as Luke opened the back door, Darlene shrieked, as if she wanted to go outside, too. The noise made Lilly cry, and the parents rushed to their babies.

Okay. Her sisters had an excuse for their restrained behavior. They had the kids to think about, and plenty of distractions just getting everyone fed and de-gooped.

Besides, they hadn't had a lot of time or energy to process this situation Josie had dropped into their laps.

Maybe Josie should talk to her father alone. She was in the mood to ask questions without restraint.

She dropped the forks into the utensil tray and dried her hands on a towel. "Excuse me, Rick. Maybe we should give the parents some time and space to settle the babies. Let's go relax."

She led her father into the living room and chose a seat near him.

After another couple of banal comments about her living-room decor, she grew weary of all the hemming and hawing. She answered Rick's question about her sofa's slipcovers and asked, "What did you think when you saw the house again? I mean, obviously we've made changes over the years, but did you realize you'd missed it? Does it bring back old memories?"

"Looks the same, but different," he said. "Didn't Isabel say she'd redone it after a flood?"

Argh. More nothing talk. "She put in new floors and countertops." Josie's voice faltered as she realized that Rick's attention drifted everywhere in the room but to her eyes.

She couldn't fathom why.

Her sisters entered the room and put the baby girls on the carpet. Lilly on her tummy—she didn't sit up yet—and Darlene next to her.

"Where are Ethan and Trevor?" Josie asked.

"Finishing the dishes," Isabel answered.

Callie sat in the chair next to Josie. "This will give us a chance to talk," she said. Although she didn't elaborate, her nod toward their father indicated that she meant it was time to get down to business.

Finally!

Unaware that he was about to be ambushed by three neglected and curious daughters, Rick eyed the baby cousins, who were obviously more taken with one another than with the rag dolls he'd brought for them. "Those are cute kids," he said. "One so much like Calliope, the other like Isabel. And I can tell you two are devoted to them. You get that from your mother."

"Thanks," Callie said. "Not to put you on the spot, Rick, but were you aware before you left that our mother wasn't quite right?"

"Elly had her faults from the day I met her, but she was a good mother." Rick firmed his mouth and stared at Callie. "She was strong-minded but sharp."

"Oh, absolutely." She shook her head. "This is so tough. I wasn't ready to meet you at all. I always figured you didn't deserve to have your daughters in your life."

He scowled. "I'm sorry you feel that way. I only left because I believed that a couple of smart little girls should learn what they could from Elly."

His defense of their mother was interesting, but Josie was stuck back on his statement: a *couple* of smart little girls?

She decided to ignore the omission. He hadn't learned of her existence until very recently and he still wasn't comfortable around her or her sisters.

"Mama wasn't people smart, though," Isabel said from her spot on the floor between the baby girls. "She acted as though she was afraid of men. She made us wary of them."

Rick studied her. "Have you girls heard your mother's history?"

"She wouldn't talk about the past," Isabel said. "She told us only that her parents had died when she was sixteen and that she had no siblings."

"That's correct," Rick said. "Her dad had a farm over near Woodbine. I lived down the road, and he hired me to help harvest his summer wheat. I was fifteen years older than Elly, but I might have been her only friend. She was pretty quiet."

"Mother was comfortable in this house with only three kids for company," Callie said. "Guess she was used to the isolation."

"That she was. When her parents died in a barn fire, she was brought to Wichita, to the home of an elderly grandfather. She finished school a year early and made her way back to Woodbine to find me. She told me she detested her grandfather—that I was the only person she really liked. That she dreamed of marrying me and starting a family."

Josie lifted her brows. "So you married her, just like that?"

Rick's face colored. "She was really pretty back then, and I suppose I was dazzled. I didn't realize until later that she saw me as a person she could manipulate."

God. That had to be the truth. Awful as it was, it

sounded typical of her mother. Josie's thoughts were echoed in the pained expressions on her sister's faces.

She hoped they'd forgive her for opening their lives to this new turmoil.

"Elly's father might have molested her," Rick said. "She never wanted to talk about him, and she wasn't a virgin on our wedding night. Maybe her grandfather hurt her that way, too. She would never say, but I had suspicions."

Josie and her sisters glanced at one another. Before anyone could speak, he continued. "But she did a good job with you girls. It does me proud to know that you two, in particular, are happy and successful." He moved his gaze between Callie and Isabel.

This time, he had no reason to leave Josie out of his story. No reason to avoid her eyes.

"Josie is happy and successful, too," Callie said. Obviously, she'd finally caught the omission. "She has tons of friends and she's working on a huge contract, decorating a series of model homes in northeast Wichita."

"That's excellent," Rick said. "I told her before, she's creative. Like Elly."

"She's also a go-getter," Isabel said. "Your visit today was mostly her doing. I mean, I'm glad I met you now, but Josie had to sell the idea to me."

Their father nodded, scowling. "That was really nice of her, then. I guess she could tell I yearned for a chance to speak to my two daughters."

Every adult in the room stilled. The only sound was a quiet rustling as Darlene tried to remove her new doll's sewn-on dress.

"Surely you meant *three* daughters," Isabel said at last.

Rick glowered at her. Isabel and Callie glared back at him.

And Josie had a moment of clarity.

Rick sat up straight in the chair, his eyes bugging out behind his glasses. "Oh!" he said, gaping at Isabel. *"Oh!"*

Immediately, Ethan and Trevor filed in, grabbed a baby each and said they'd bundle the girls in their coats and go out to the yard to play with Luke. Apparently, they'd heard at least part of the conversation from the kitchen.

"Well. I suppose I didn't make myself clear before," Rick said.

"Try again," Callie said calmly.

"When I left, your mother was pregnant."

Callie frowned at him, apparently believing he was just a confused old man.

But something else was happening. Josie recognized that now. She sat bracing herself, anticipating the jolt of news she didn't want to hear after all.

"But we hadn't been together in that way for over a year," Rick finished.

Of course.

He'd said that before, during her second visit to Woodbine. Now it made sense. Josie waited, completely focused on the words that would likely change her view of the world from here on out.

"Elly and I had been fighting. We couldn't afford a third baby and she was set on a dozen." He chuckled humorlessly. "Even if she'd won the argument, I

didn't…you know. The baby couldn't have been mine."
He shook his head.

"Our mother seldom even spoke to anyone," Callie argued, her face pale. "Especially not to men. She wouldn't have had an affair, if that's what you're suggesting."

Rick met her gaze. "I wouldn't have thought so, either."

Callie, Isabel and Josie all glanced at one another, communicating pain and wonder in their expressions. Callie's and Isabel's faces also showed sympathy.

They were getting it now.

Josie wasn't their full sister.

"I thought she might have done something stupid that day," Rick said. "She went into town by herself."

He was looking at Josie now. Focusing on her alone for the first time. He was letting her know: this was her story to hear.

She nodded, prompting him to continue.

"She didn't usually like to go out at all. She sent me. For some reason that day, she said she had a hankering to go into town without the kids. She wanted to shop. She was getting stronger, she insisted." He paused, shaking his head again. "She was gone three hours."

"That wouldn't necessarily mean anything," Callie said.

"Believe me, I told myself that. For a while. Then she started smiling for no reason. She'd rest a hand on her belly. When she dug out her maternity clothes and said she was just getting fat, I was almost certain. Elly had a thin frame. Only got big when she was pregnant."

"Why didn't you ask her?" Josie asked.

He didn't hesitate. "She'd have bitten my head off. Actually, her attacks were already increasing. I couldn't challenge her without getting into some God-awful clash in front of you kids. I had to leave."

Josie didn't need to question him further. Now she knew. She felt different because she *was* different. Everything made perfect sense.

But Rick kept talking. "I found work with a buddy up in Woodbine. I thought it was the only way." He studied Josie. "I'd be proud to be your father," he murmured. "I'm just not."

After a moment that felt endless, Josie felt Callie's hands on her arms. Her oldest sister—good God, her *half* sister—pulled her out of the chair. "Come here, hon."

They exchanged a long hug, then Callie took her hand and led her into the kitchen. "You okay?" she whispered as they stood near the table.

"Sure. I'm—" She broke off and simply nodded. Then she moved backward, deciding she'd sit, and nearly missed the chair.

Callie caught her and helped her, then crouched in front of Josie. "Well, I'm stunned, hon. I had no idea."

Josie sighed, then ran the side of her hand against eyes that threatened to water.

She wouldn't cry.

"I can't understand how I could have met him twice without figuring it out," she said, trying to smile. "What an idiot!"

"He never told you," Callie said as she sat cross-legged on the floor in front of Josie. "He thought you knew or something. Didn't Gabe go with you the last time?"

Gabe.

God. Things had been so odd between her and Gabe. After that kiss, she'd been unsure about how to talk to him. She'd avoided him, using the excuse that she was swamped with dinner preparations. That she was worried about Lilly and also the strangeness between her and her father.

All true. All still excuses.

What could she say to Gabe? They'd indulged, and long enough that their kiss couldn't be considered an "Oops, was that you?" mistake. Perhaps they'd mention the experience eventually, probably in a joking way.

Remember the time we slipped?

Something was changing between them. Whether or not they should get involved physically, they were more involved emotionally. She figured she should let all this other turmoil die down and then contemplate how to handle this new complication between her and Gabe.

And then again, she wished he were here right now.

"Yes, Gabe went with me," she said to Callie.

"He must not have known, either. Right?"

Josie thought about Gabe's reactions at Rick's house. "No, he couldn't have known, or he'd have realized that I didn't. He'd have told me."

She bit her lip, remembering about her abruptness with Gabe over the phone this week. Was she exactly like her mother? She sure as heck wasn't like Rick Blume.

Small wonder.

"This explains a lot, doesn't it?" Josie said.

"What do you mean?"

"You and Izzy are tall and quiet. I'm chunky and loud."

Callie lifted herself onto her knees and caught Josie's eye. "You're gorgeous and vivacious. I've always envied your curves."

Josie studied Callie. Her sisters had been dead on, she realized. They might all have been better off if she'd heeded their mother's warnings concerning their father.

She'd have been better off.

Now she'd lost another piece of her identity—she was only Callie and Isabel's half sister, and she still had no clue about her real dad.

"She wanted a baby," Josie said, laughing hoarsely as she thought about it again. "Can you imagine our mother doing that? Going to town to find some guy and get pregnant?"

"No." Now Callie moved up to a chair next to Josie's. "I suppose I can understand her desperation, though. I felt it, to some degree, before I had Luke."

"I'm not sure I understand any of it," Josie said. "Why wouldn't Mother have told us? Told *me*."

"I'd guess she was embarrassed," Callie said. "Maybe even ashamed, as much as Mama could feel shame. And I want to believe that she wanted you to feel as much a part of the family as any of us. You are, of course. As much family as me or Isabel. Please believe that."

"I'm not even your whole sister."

"Shhh! Josie. Think about it," Callie said. "Think

about the way I feel about Luke. The way Lilly and Luke are, together."

Her sister was right, Josie realized. Luke was Callie's child through love. Ethan had fathered him, but Callie had been unable to conceive. She'd tried a lot of things, and had eventually used an egg donor. In the four years between babies, infertility researchers had advanced the science enough that Callie had been able to get pregnant naturally the last time.

Lilly had Callie's blond hair and fair complexion, while Luke was a miniature Ethan. Yet it was obvious that Callie loved Luke as much as Lilly. And baby Lilly lit up around her brother. She probably always would.

Perhaps this new knowledge didn't have to change Josie's entire view of the world. Luke was as much Callie's child as Lilly was, even if the biological tie was missing. Perhaps Josie could view her situation in the same way.

"You okay?" Callie asked softly.

Josie chuckled again, a wild, crazy sound to match her mood. This news was just another twist in a world that had felt completely out of whack for a while now. "I'll *be* okay," she said. "Sometime."

"What would help you feel better?" Callie asked. "Can I help?"

Callie had enough going on in her own life. Lilly hadn't had another episode since last Saturday, but Callie and Ethan hated the thought of their daughter remaining in a drug-fogged state. They were exhausting themselves, searching for answers.

It had been great of them to come to Josie's lasagna dinner. It was wonderful of Callie to focus on Josie now, even for a moment.

"I know what *won't* help me feel better," Josie said.

Callie frowned the question.

"I don't want to go into that living room to visit politely with Rick Blume. And I don't want to hear any more explanations for his neglect of any of us. Not today."

Josie would get acquainted with Rick Blume, if only because he was her sisters' father. Callie and Isabel would decide how much or how little to include him in their lives, and Josie would be gracious.

Just not today.

"I'd like to get away from here for a while. Do you mind if I leave you here with him?" Josie nodded toward the living room, where Rick waited with Isabel. "Though it doesn't seem fair for me to impose his presence on you, and then leave."

"I understand why you need to go. And I'm glad you contacted Rick. I think we'll all eventually be glad we met him."

"Hope so." Josie grabbed her truck keys and driver's license from her catchall drawer, then pulled her sweater from the back of her chair.

"What are you going to do now, Josie?"

"Escape. Drive. Think." Josie struggled to put on the sweater. "I'm not really sure."

Callie helped Josie find her second sleeve. "Okay. Just…well, whatever you do, remember we're still your family—me and Ethan, Izzy and Trevor, the kids. We all love you as much as ever."

And she loved them, perhaps more than ever.

But right now, she craved a comfort none of them could give her.

Chapter Seven

Ignoring the scrape of a branch against the window, Gabe squinted down at the old beech hand plane he'd found at an auction. He wiped away a thin layer of unidentifiable gunk, then dropped the rag to study the fine old tool.

He'd bought the plane with a box of miscellaneous tools this autumn, and he'd been itching to sort through the collection for weeks.

There was that sound again. It was more a ping than a scratch, as if it was beginning to sleet. Gabe glanced out the second-story bedroom window. It was clear outside, but he knew it was growing colder. He'd framed in a couple of bedrooms on the Kramer job today, and every time he'd had to go out to grab more wood, he'd noticed a temperature drop.

Okay. That sound was too systematic to be the wind. Either some squirrel had developed great aim and was trying to lure him outside, or someone was out there. Gabe set the plane aside and strode to the window.

Josie was in the drive, peering up at the lit window.

She had her arms wrapped around her chest, she was clutching something bright orange and she was bouncing.

She must have been out there awhile.

Gabe pointed toward the back door.

As he left the room and rushed down the stairs, he wondered about what might have brought her here. Tonight was her big dinner with Rick Blume, Gabe was certain. He wouldn't have confused the dates. She'd been frantically busy with preparations, and wound up a little tighter every time he'd called her.

On his way through the hallway to the back door, he glanced at the grandfather clock in the foyer. It was just after seven o'clock. She and her family would barely have finished their dinner.

After he'd yanked the door open and motioned her inside, he asked, "Don't you have a houseful of guests?"

She handed him the orange thing—his plastic-wrapped newspaper—and instead of answering said, "Why's this still out there?"

He dropped it on a hall table. "Because I worked all day and came home intent on eating something and working upstairs."

"Your door was locked."

"You have a key."

She glared at him, her mouth set in a stubborn line and her eyes huge. If Gabe guessed correctly, Josie was sitting on an overabundance of emotions.

Blast it, he wanted to kiss away her upset. Make her forget whatever had happened at her dinner and think about him. About how things had shifted between them.

Didn't she realize how important that was?

"I forgot to bring my key," she said in a voice that was calmer now. "You afraid of the boogeyman or something?"

He was glad to hear that she had her sense of humor, even if she wasn't ready to talk. "I locked the door because I wasn't planning on going out again."

"It's 7:10."

"Mmm-hmm."

"You calling it a night at 7:10?"

Josie might be maturing, but sometimes their age difference still gaped. She'd swear that now was prime time to get out in the world. Gabe loved these quiet evenings, when all he had to do was putter.

And Josie knew that. "I've been busy upstairs."

"Doing what?"

"Cleaning some auction items."

"Can I help?"

Oh, yeah. She was in another funk. Not ready to talk, but needing his company. "Only if you answer me this, Josie. Did your guests leave?"

"Beats me."

As if her retort explained her presence here, Josie walked past him into his mudroom. After shrugging out of the sweater that couldn't have been warm enough, she draped it over a wall peg and continued inside. "You up in the granny room?"

"I am."

Gabe lived here alone, about three miles north of Augusta in a too-large house with a back patio overlooking the vast Kansas sunsets. When he'd given Josie her first tour of his place, she'd named the rooms according to how she thought they'd be used by the next owners.

Although she claimed that he bought and sold houses as fast as he bought and sold cars, he'd moved only twice in the past four years. Someday when he found the time, he'd build his dream home and stay.

Josie had dubbed his biggest spare the granny room because of the ancient, pink-rosebud wallpaper and because the smaller, blue-painted room next to it would work well as a nursery. Gabe had left those rooms as he'd found them, but he'd had Josie help him redo a too frilly master bedroom and bath. They'd stripped the wallpaper and slapped on deep red paint. They'd installed new, masculine fixtures. Gabe had also moved a portion of the bedroom wall to enlarge an inadequate shower enclosure, and Josie had found him a black claw-foot tub that would easily fit two.

While they'd worked, Josie had begun referring to his bathroom as the Sin Suite. The trouble was, Josie had always coveted that bathtub. If he invited a woman into it, he'd feel as if he was cheating. No sins had been executed there.

Even now as Gabe followed Josie upstairs, he fought an image of her turning the wrong way, entering that very room to christen the tub in more ways than one.

After their kiss—their first *real* kiss—the idea wasn't inconceivable. But she was obviously confused about things. He wouldn't push.

Josie veered right, entering the granny room. Immediately, she claimed the folding chair he'd been using.

Picking up an antique handsaw he'd left on a bench, she said, "What do you use to clean this?"

Gabe handed her a bottle of mineral spirits and a rag. He pulled an old stool from the closet, planted it across the bench from Josie, then sat and returned his attention to the hand plane. She'd talk when she was ready.

Kiss when she was ready, too.

She cleared her throat, her fingers poised on the cap of the bottle. "Why on earth don't you do this out in your garage?" she asked.

He glanced up. "Cold out there."

"Then I guess you're planning on recarpeting in here," she said. "Hope Granny won't mind if I ruin the mauve flowers."

He didn't smile. Josie hadn't managed to find humor in her own quip. "Just be careful."

She started working. Ten minutes later, she dropped the newly cleaned saw on the bench and looked at Gabe. "He's not my dad."

She'd sounded so matter-of-fact. Perhaps he'd heard her wrong. "I beg your pardon?"

"Rick Blume. He said I couldn't be his daughter."

Her words had been dully spoken, her face expressionless except for a fierce little thrust of her chin. Poor stubborn, sweet kid.

Gabe set down the plane between them and stepped around the bench to pull her into his embrace. She fit in his arms as if made for them. If he'd denied that possibility before, he couldn't now.

"He said my mother went into town one day just to get pregnant." Josie's voice was muffled against his shoulder. "He left because she was pregnant with another man's child. I'm not his kid."

Damn it, the rumors had been true.

Right now, Gabe felt as if he had been the one to hurt Josie. He'd suspected the possibility that she wasn't Rick's child, and he hadn't warned her. He'd prayed it wasn't true. Or, more accurately, he'd prayed that she'd never find out, one way or another.

Now the best he could do was to comfort her, so he kept holding her. Eventually, he realized he was sweaty and full of sawdust and God knows what else. He thought of that tub again and felt like a world-class jerk.

He backed up immediately, but when he saw the blind pain in Josie's eyes he wanted to close his.

He felt so guilty. So sad for her. And helpless.

He hoped Josie and her sisters would never find out that this big news wasn't news at all to a lot of people in Augusta. Or to him.

Josie managed a cheeky grin. "Hey! Now don't *you* get upset. I'm fine." She swiveled toward the door. "Mind if I grab a beer from your fridge?"

"Not at all."

"Want one?"

Oh, yeah. Good idea. The two of them could get good and tanked, then he could tell her about a certain bathtub fantasy. Or about how he had suspected all along that she might be searching for the wrong man.

"No, you go ahead."

After Josie had wandered away, Gabe poked around in the box of tools and thought about those stories.

He'd actually heard them years ago. From friends. From friends' parents. Even from his own mother. She hadn't been spreading gossip maliciously, though. She'd simply been interested in knowing enough about Gabe's new friend to speak to her without offending her.

She'd hinted that there was more to the story than speculation about Josie's parentage, but she hadn't wanted to repeat it. And when she'd asked Gabe to keep what she'd told him in trust, he'd been relieved. He'd hoped that Josie would never unearth any of it.

Now he wondered if that long-ago decision was going to come back and bite him on the butt.

Josie walked in with her beer. After taking the folding chair again, she picked up the plane and turned it over in her hand. "This one's nice."

"Notice the lines on the woodwork." Gabe pointed at some of the markings, taking care not to touch her. He might be a guy in lust with Josie, but he was also her friend.

"It's funny," Josie said. "You buy new cars and houses every couple of years, yet you have such a love for old gadgets and tools."

"It's the craftsmanship. It reminds me to slow down and put my heart and soul into the projects I build."

She laid down the piece and sipped her drink as she perused the contents of the box. "This isn't a wood-working tool." She drew out a rusted garden spade.

"That's from your house," he said. "I found it in the shed after the flood and Izzy gave it to me. It must have belonged to your mother."

As she eyed the tool, Josie clenched and unclenched her jaw. Then she put the beer to her lips and let it rest there for two seconds before putting it back down. "It all makes sense now, doesn't it?" she said.

"What does, Josie?"

"The differences. Callie and Isabel favor Mother, at least in appearance. I must resemble whoever the heck it was my mother found in town that day. Or no one."

Gabe kept his gaze steady on hers.

She set the bottle on his workbench. "You aren't surprised, are you?"

He froze.

What did she mean? Did she suspect that he'd known? How?

She snorted. "You must have seen the same things I have. My build. My personality. You can't be surprised that I'm not Callie and Isabel's full sister."

Oh. She wasn't accusing him of protecting the big secret. She was telling him that he should have suspected, as she had, that she was different for a reason. He really needed to grab his wits and hang on tight.

"In retrospect, it makes sense," he said. "Do you think your sisters will stay in touch with Rick now?"

"Maybe. He's their dad, and he was attentive to the kids today. Luke called him Poppy once, and Darlene sat on his lap without crying. I believe they'll get along. I just don't know how hard they'll pursue the relationship."

"Do you feel left out?"

"Only time will tell how I feel about all of this." She offered a tiny chuckle. "But I'll be okay."

"That's right, and don't you forget it."

Gabe tried not to envision the hundred ways he could get her mind off tonight's news. The hundred places in this house alone they could try.

She scanned the box again. "Is there something else you want cleaned?"

Her voice sounded shaky and small.

"Josie."

She sniffed as she plucked out a card of old buttons and flipped them over in her palm. She dropped them in the box, then turned her back to him and lifted her hand briefly to her face.

Wiping away tears?

"Hey, kid." He approached from behind her, moving a hand to her shoulder to tug her around. He hauled her into his arms, no thinking required. He cared for Josie in this way. He had for a long time.

But she responded differently.

She moved closer, nuzzling her mouth against the side of his neck. Even kissing him there.

His body began to prime.

Some switch that had been tightened into an Off position had loosened, and he thought about sex with Josie too often these days. But he wasn't sure if she was even aware of her actions.

She kept kissing, inching her lips along his jaw until her mouth was next to his. He glanced—she had her eyes shut—and then he gave in.

He kissed Josie again the way he wanted to.

This kiss heated quickly. Every slight change he made—slanting his mouth, shifting his hands, involving his tongue—was met by an equally bold move on Josie's part.

They kissed for an endless time that made him more certain that Josie—his good friend Josie—might be the woman he'd want at his deathbed.

When he felt her hands slide around his torso and climb his chest until she fingered his top button—she was pondering the idea of continuing, he was certain— he met her gaze with a sober look.

Gabe the man wanted her to yank the buttons from his shirt. He'd only make quicker work of hers.

Gabe the friend wanted Josie to be sure.

She stopped. Scrutinized his chest with lowered brows and let out a soft snort. Then she leaned forward until her forehead rested against that same button.

And she started laughing.

Gabe laughed, too, for a long time. Eventually, the chuckles subsided and he held her quietly. "What's going on in that head of yours?" he murmured a moment later.

She kept her face pressed against his shirt. "Wish I could figure that out."

"Look at me, Josie."

She did, and damn if her eyes weren't teary again. "I will be okay, right?"

"You bet you will." He tugged her close, kissed her temple.

And kept the night sane.

FOUR EVENINGS LATER, Gabe sat with his bare feet propped across his coffee table as he tried to get his sister's teacher friend to quit babbling and hang up. When they'd never connected after his mother's Halloween party, Shelby Roberts had started calling him.

He hadn't spelled things out to her. He'd hate for her to report back to Nadine that he was involved with Josie when he was only adjusting to the idea himself. But Shelby wasn't getting his "not-interested" messages, either.

She'd just asked him to go to her cousin's holiday dinner. She claimed that she couldn't stand going alone again this year, and that from Nadine's description, she thought Gabe had sounded like exactly the sort of man she should meet. She hoped he'd do her this favor. After taking a deep breath, she started listing the reasons a holiday-dinner first date was a good idea.

Gabe's doorbell rang—twice. He got up, phone to ear, and flipped on his porch light. He squinted out the peephole.

It was Josie again.

Grimacing as Shelby continued, Gabe opened his front door and indicated with a crook of his head that Josie should come inside.

"Are you okay, Gabe? You sound distracted," Shelby said.

No kidding.

Tomboy Josie looked distinctly female in a thigh-length leather coat that emphasized a set of sizzling, stocking-clad legs. Made him wonder what Josie had on underneath.

Made him imagine her *wearing* nothing underneath.

"Hey, Shelby. I've got to go. It's late."

"My word, I just checked my watch. Is it really after ten?" Shelby said, then immediately returned to her gabbing. Gabe couldn't say about what. He caught Josie's eye, lifting a finger to indicate that he'd get off the phone shortly, then swiveled away from her to close his door.

He tried to nudge a second goodbye attempt into Shelby's new diatribe about her students' late bedtimes, while Josie moved around behind him.

A whoosh and plop meant that Josie had wriggled out of that coat, but by the time he'd turned around she'd disappeared into his kitchen. She clicked across the tile—must be wearing some kind of fancy shoes—and the light came on in there. The clicks stopped. He pictured her standing at his patio doors, checking out the western sky.

Had something else happened to upset her?

"So you'll do it? Oh! I'm so glad," Shelby said.

Blast it, what had he just agreed to do? He heard Josie open his refrigerator door. "Uh, don't ink me in for that just yet," he told Shelby. "I can't decide until I get details. Talk to you later."

"But I just told you. We're all going to—"

Gabe heard Shelby's voice in the earpiece as he hung up. My God. According to Nadine, Shelby Roberts was a great teacher and wonderful person. She was supposed to be blond, bubbly and beautiful. Nadine's six-year-old, Tyler, had a huge crush on the reading teacher.

Gabe only knew that she babbled.

He went into his kitchen and found Josie, still

standing in front of his open refrigerator door. She watched him come in, albeit vacantly, then lifted a beer from the door rack. "D'ya mind?"

"Not at all."

When she lifted a second bottle and gave him a questioning look, he shook his head.

She opened the cap, took a sip and closed the refrigerator door. She maneuvered around until she could lean against that same door, allowing her head to rest against the black steel surface, and flicked her eyes from his mouth to his chest to his feet,

Focusing now, on him.

"Hey, Gabe," she said, her voice low. Needy, somehow.

Did she know the crazy thoughts she kindled with two words? Gabe could imagine waking up to that intimate greeting every morning.

He moved nearer, stopping a couple feet in front of her, curious about her reaction.

Josie's eyes followed his movements, but she remained still, simply taking him in.

He did the same, and sweet Lord she was white-hot in her tiny red skirt and jacket. She drifted forward as though caught in his spell, then teetered in those shoes.

Gabe was unable to resist any longer. He looped a hand behind her waist and tugged her into his arms.

He meant to hug her, but she tipped her head up to offer lips. Even then he might have pecked and retreated, but she responded.

Damn, did she respond. Beautifully.

She even stood on tiptoe to gain better access, initiating a game of tongue-tag. Gabe slid his hands down to her bottom, bracing her.

The feel of that pliant flesh beneath his hands—the very thought that he was cupping her derriere—had him imagining her naked.

His arousal thickened and throbbed. He yanked Josie closer and hoped to hell she'd arrived to demand sex from him.

Now.

Right here in front of his fridge.

Josie was no prude. She'd made it clear since forever that she liked sex and men, probably in that order. At the moment it hardly mattered. He could cover both.

But she backed up, lifting the beer bottle as if to fend him off with it. "Gabe! What was that for?"

Of course, between the two of them things had to be more complicated. He shifted uncomfortably. Fought for control. And for breath. "Just a hello, I guess."

"Mmm. Well, hello to you, too." She shot a glance toward the bulge in his pants, then surprised him by blushing.

He wouldn't remind her that she'd already greeted him, in that moment stirring his desire.

He'd moved too fast. That was all there was to it.

Gabe let his gaze fall to Josie's chest and linger on a shiny black jacket button he'd love to undo. "Where've you been, dressed like that?"

"Work."

That explained the sharp getup. He leaned against the counter. Yanked his eyes and mind off Josie's chest.

Off thoughts of sex. Onto anything else. "Peter Kramer was supposed to visit your site today, wasn't he?"

"Yes."

"Did he like what you've done with the model home?"

"He said he did. Said the circular fireplace was inspired. Said he'd have to hide the maple bookcases from his wife or she'd want a pair in their family room at home."

"Good. I was confident that he'd like your work."

"Well, thanks for the referral." Josie regarded the beer bottle as if surprised to find it in her hand. She'd taken one drink.

Now she pulled out a stool and sat at Gabe's breakfast nook. Instead of guzzling the drink, as he expected, she toyed with the frost on the bottle. "I drove up to Woodbine," she said.

"Today?"

She nodded.

"Last I heard, you were planning to say goodbye to Izzy and Trevor this morning and head off to a long day of work. Didn't you have a lot of catch-up to do?"

"I did. I worked until six-thirty and then drove straight up to Rick and Brenda's place. I just got back."

"Why'd you go this time?" Gabe asked. Unnecessarily, since he could predict her answer.

"To ask who he was."

Gabe didn't ask who she was referring to. Good heavens. Josie was still hunting for her father.

He wondered at the chances of convincing her that she should stop looking and be happy. And he kept wrestling with the thought that they should talk about what was happening between them.

He recognized that Josie was going through a rough time. So much was happening at once. Would she wake up some morning and wonder how the two of them had gotten involved?

Was he taking advantage of her vulnerability?

He'd need to be careful. Maybe this was why his gut had always told him it was a mistake to get involved with his best friend.

"Did you learn anything?" he asked.

"Rick remembered a first name. He said this guy was a handyman who'd been to the house a couple of times. He figured it was the only person who made sense."

Ella had always been described as a woman with a distrust of all things unfamiliar. A dislike for all things male. "Just some handyman? That doesn't sound right."

Josie smiled. "The guy's name was Joe."

"Wow."

She lifted the bottle halfway to her mouth, then set it down again. But Josie said nothing.

"So what are you thinking?"

She stared at her beer a moment, then got up to return the nearly full drink to his fridge minus its cap. "Let's go," she said.

Her heels clicked purposefully against Gabe's kitchen tiles, then silenced when she reached the thick carpeting of his living room.

"Where're we headed?" he asked as he followed.

"Rick didn't want to tell me, but Brenda hinted that this Joe guy might have hung out at Mary's once upon a time." Josie stopped near his sofa and picked up her coat.

"*Our* Mary's?"

"Yes."

"The bar here in Augusta where we shoot pool?"

"That'd be the one."

"Wow."

She slid into her coat. "So let's go."

Was she planning to search for the man tonight? Most of Augusta would be at home or even asleep. Those who were out would likely not welcome company or questions. Even if it were daylight, Gabe wasn't certain he was ready to pursue this father search with Josie. The man may have come and gone from town within a one-day period back in 1980.

Or he might still be here. And Josie might be hurt.

"Uh, if you didn't notice, I'm not dressed."

She was buttoning into her coat, but she glanced at his sleep pants. Those hazel eyes widened.

Did Gabe see heat in them? If he did, it was gone in a flash.

"Then go get something on."

Gabe crossed his arms in front of him and stared at her, unmoving. "What're you planning, kid?"

"I want you to take me to Mary's. I can talk to people, see if anyone remembers this guy."

"Tonight? But it's late. You only just got home. Give it time."

"You want me to go alone?"

He moved his gaze to that coat. To the sexy legs under that coat. His first thought when he'd seen Josie in that coat and stockings was sex. Second and third thoughts, too.

Hard to imagine that every man at Mary's tonight would think differently. "Hell, no. You can't go alone."

She eyed Gabe's pants again. "Then get dressed."

The knowledge of where her gaze rested caused Gabe's body to harden again—instantly.

Curse his bad timing, anyway.

Before she noticed, Gabe started up the stairs. "If I remember right, Mary's has changed hands at least five times since I've been old enough to go to bars," he hollered over his shoulder. "No one'll remember anything."

Josie didn't answer.

Despite the fact that he was upstairs and across the house from her, Gabe closed his bedroom door. He went in the bathroom to splash cold water on his face and torso, encouraging rapid cooling, then he glanced in the mirror to check the whisker situation. His beard didn't look as bad as it felt.

When he saw the reflection of that decadent clawfoot tub, he sighed. Clearly, tonight wasn't the night to christen the blamed thing properly.

He wasn't sure that night would ever arrive.

Moments later, he had on some jeans and was carrying his socks and running shoes down to the living room, where Josie stood in the entry, tapping a pointy-toed shoe against the carpet. "The manager might have records about who owned the place back then," she said, as if they'd never paused their conversation.

He glanced at her as he sat on the sofa to yank on his socks. "Maybe. Maybe not."

He'd just started tying the first shoelace, when she

opened the front door. "Hurry, would you? I'll wait outside."

Gabe made quick work of the other shoe, then grabbed his coat and slammed out the door. She had her truck running, so he got in and buckled up. "We can talk to whoever's working at Mary's," he said. "I'm sure that's your best bet. But if nothing pans out we'll come straight home. We're both putting in long work hours. We have no business chasing around town this late."

"Really?" she asked. "Wasn't that you who stayed at Callie and Ethan's until midnight on Sunday?"

"I was invited."

"It *was* midnight when you left, though, right?" she asked. "You can handle another late night."

He rolled his eyes in the darkness of the truck cab. "I just don't want to show up at Mary's, hear the manager say some guy named Joe used to eat at the Dairy Queen and then we race over there. Okay? Let this be it for now."

She was turning onto Ohio Street and didn't answer.

It had taken Josie all of two minutes to get to Mary's. It took her two seconds to yank her keys from her ignition and get out.

Gabe's legs were much longer than hers, yet he fell a couple of paces behind her in the lot. "Why are you in such a damn hurry?" he hollered after her.

"I just want to know."

"I get that. Just…slow down."

"Why?"

She was already headed inside, but he'd have had plenty of answers for her if she'd cared to listen.

OFFICIAL OPINION POLL

ANSWER 3 QUESTIONS AND WE'LL SEND YOU
2 FREE BOOKS AND A FREE GIFT!

0074823 |||||||||||| |||||||| |||||||| **FREE GIFT CLAIM #** 3953

YOUR OPINION COUNTS!

Please check TRUE or FALSE below to express your opinion about the following statements:

Q1 Do you believe in "true love"?

"TRUE LOVE HAPPENS ONLY ONCE IN A LIFETIME." ○ TRUE ○ FALSE

Q2 Do you think marriage has any value in today's world?

"YOU CAN BE TOTALLY COMMITTED TO SOMEONE WITHOUT BEING MARRIED." ○ TRUE ○ FALSE

Q3 What kind of books do you enjoy?

"A GREAT NOVEL MUST HAVE A HAPPY ENDING." ○ TRUE ○ FALSE

YES, I have scratched the area below.

Please send me the 2 FREE BOOKS and FREE GIFT for which I qualify. I understand I am under no obligation to purchase any books, as explained on the back of this card.

354 HDL EFWV   154 HDL EFVL

FIRST NAME   LAST NAME

ADDRESS

APT.#   CITY

STATE/PROV.   ZIP/POSTAL CODE

www.eHarlequin.com

(HTF-AR-06/06)

Offer limited to one per household and not valid to current Harlequin American Romance® subscribers. All orders subject to approval. Credit or Debit balances in a customer's account(s) may be offset by any other outstanding balance owed by or to the customer. Please allow 4 to 6 weeks for delivery.

The Harlequin Reader Service® — Here's how it works:

Accepting your 2 free books and mystery gift places you under no obligation to buy anything. You may keep the books and gift and return the shipping statement marked "cancel." If you do not cancel, about a month later we'll send you 4 additional books and bill you just $4.24 each in the U.S., or $4.99 each in Canada, plus 25¢ shipping & handling per book and applicable taxes if any.* That's the complete price and – compared to cover prices of $4.99 each in the U.S., and $5.99 each in Canada – it's quite a bargain! You may cancel at any time, but if you choose to continue, every month we'll send you 4 more books which you may either purchase at the discount price or return to us and cancel your subscription.

*Terms and prices subject to change without notice. Sales tax applicable in N.Y. Canadian residents will be charged applicable provincial taxes and GST.

She couldn't have had time to think about what could happen if she did find this man. Perhaps Ella Blume had confused her thoughts about Rick and about Josie's biological father. If this Joe, or whoever, was just some fool her mother had used during one fateful afternoon, maybe he'd been the drunken bum the girls had heard about.

Josie didn't need that kind of trouble in her life.

But if she was hell-bent on inviting it in, Gabe couldn't let her do so alone.

Chapter Eight

As soon as Josie had entered the pub and scanned the darkened room, her stomach tied into knots. Mary's looked like the same smoky bar where she'd hung out nearly once a week for years, except it was almost empty. Somehow she knew she'd expected too much.

Had she hoped to see a neon sign blinking J-O-E above an old man's head? Nothing that blatant, yet not the same shabby, local beer joint. Not the same weary patrons.

One of those regulars sat hunched over a half-empty glass at the bar, staring up at the television as Jay Leno talked to Uma Thurman. Two other men played a game of pool. A few couples cozied up in the booths, but no one else was here. Even the barkeep had gone missing.

An employee was probably her best bet for information. Gabe had been right about that. Josie hung her coat on a rack near the door, then approached the bar.

"Have you seen the bartender?" she asked the old guy.

The man glanced over his shoulder at her, then scanned the area behind the bar. "She was right here a while ago. Don't know where she went. Been watchin' Leno."

The television lured the man's attention. He laughed with the audience at some crack Leno had made.

"Can I bother you with one more question?"

"Whatzat?"

"Have you been coming around here a long time? Would you know anyone who used to come here? A customer? A man, maybe close to your age?"

He turned to her, suspicion dark on his face. He lifted his martini glass. "Here for this. Not socializin'."

She eyed his drink. "And you're not Joe, are you?"

"Hell, no. Name's Earl." The man stared at the television again, already focusing on it.

She knew it was stupid, but she felt so deflated.

She'd been stunned by Rick's confession that he might know her father's identity, even though she'd gone to Woodbine to beg for clues. The man's name, Joe, and the fact that he'd frequented Mary's had made Josie feel as if things were clicking into place.

As if she was meant to discover everything tonight.

Or to even find this Joe.

Gabe approached minus his coat, and Josie noticed the expression of caution in his eyes.

"Don't say it," she said. "I already realize I was silly to rush over here."

He rested a hand on the small of her waist and pulled her to his side. "It's Tuesday night after a holiday weekend, Josie. Everyone's home recovering."

"Guess so." She nodded toward the pool players. "Would it be completely idiotic to ask them?"

He studied the three guys, all in their twenties or thirties. "Ask them what?"

It was idiotic. But Josie was determined to learn anything she could. "If they know the history of this place," she said. "If their mothers or fathers frequented Mary's and might recollect a Joe who probably visited here, once upon a time."

She chuckled at the absurdity of what she'd just said. "God, I must be really tired."

With a nudge at her back, Gabe propelled Josie toward the pool table. "Don't worry about it, kid. We're here. You might as well ask whoever you want."

Of course, the pool players remembered nothing about some bar visitor from several decades ago. The couples in the booths weren't any more help. Several of them pointed out that they hadn't even been born at the time.

"I still say your best bet's someone who works here," Gabe said. "Even then it's a long shot."

Josie waved toward the bar. "The bartender's missing, and Earl, there, has no clue where she went."

Gabe motioned toward an empty booth. "We don't have to rush out of here. Let's wait. The bartender can't have gone far and she might know enough to give us a start. Augusta's small enough that the bar crowd probably gets pretty familiar."

Josie slid onto the vinyl seat, then scooted farther in when Gabe climbed in on the same side—something he'd never done before.

"Know what else I think?" he asked.

"Why am I certain you're about to tell me?"

He backed up a little, grinning at her joke, then

quickly sobered. "Maybe it's good that we have to wait. Before you continue this hunt, you need to think about who this man might be. He could be anyone, Josie. You realize that?"

"He was a handyman. Someone my mother knew as an acquaintance, at least. I've told you all this."

"Simple facts." Gabe rested a hand against her thigh. "You should consider what kind of man would do what he did. Your mother, who was notorious for being tough, must have made a play for him."

Josie snorted at the thought.

"He slept with her," Gabe continued. "If they were only acquaintances, it means something. If he was more to her, somehow, it means something else. I'm not sure he comes out ahead, either way."

"Yeah, well. News flash, Gabe. Lots of guys do things like that. Some can be real sleazes. Does it matter at this point?"

Gabe moved his hand away from her leg and folded it with his other on the tabletop. He shifted away from her.

"Josie." He said one word only, but much more with his tone. Depending on the moment, that tone could bring her to her senses or make her mad.

Josie wriggled farther into the booth and pressed her back against the wall so she could see his expressions. "Why are you discouraging me from searching for my father, Gabe?"

He cocked his head, as if thinking about it. "Well, your purpose for finding him was to learn about Lilly's genetic background." He lifted his shoulders. "You did that when you spoke to Rick. Callie is investigating bio-chemical causes for the seizures, right? She and Ethan are meeting with this new neurologist?"

"Right."

"So why continue? Why open your life to pain? Your mother warned you."

"I need questions answered for myself, too. Partly because of mother's warnings. I wonder what she was hiding."

Gabe's jaw worked, but he didn't say anything. Both of them scanned the bar, where nothing had changed. Old Earl kept watching Leno. The pool players kept playing.

Mary's appeared to be running itself.

"Maybe this is as good a time as any to talk about something else," Gabe said. "Have you thought about the other change in your life?"

Oh, God. He'd bring that up now? "Change?" she asked.

"Us."

Josie studied his fingers, folded together on the table in front of them. Those hands that had grabbed her butt a few short minutes ago.

Her yearning for him had been so violent. She'd felt his arousal, and she'd ached to drag him into her bed-room and take him on.

To feel his body inside hers. To touch him. To taste him. To reach for that sweet release, with him.

With Gabe. Her best friend. Her brick.

No, she hadn't let herself think about it. Not really.

And she couldn't now. Not now, when she felt such a frantic need to find this man who could be her father.

"Gabe, get on your side."

"What?"

She stuck her elbow in his ribs. "Move to the other side of the booth. You're making me claustrophobic and I can't see your reactions."

He hesitated for a second, then slipped out and back in across from her. Where he'd sat dozens of times, probably in this same booth. The expression on his face had sure changed, though. He looked…upset? Sad?

"Too much is happening at once," she explained. "I don't know what I think about anything."

Just that she couldn't lose Gabe, and that starting meant they were on their way to finishing.

Gabe opened his mouth at the same time that the sound system came on—loud. An old Jimmy Buffett song blared into the room. Gabe closed his mouth and scowled toward the bar, and Josie decided she could go for a margarita about now.

Hey! She hadn't noticed till this moment, but the music hadn't been playing in Mary's before. Then she realized that the bartender, a busty brunette Josie recognized, had reappeared near the deejay station. The woman examined the stereo system, scratched her temple and then fiddled with some dial. The volume of the music lessened, then the bartender strode across the space and bustled past the bar's swing door. She shook her head as she made some comment to the Leno fan.

Josie caught Gabe's gaze for a moment before dropping hers. "The music's my cue, bud." She noted that he didn't smile at her joke, then left the booth.

Gabe could follow if he wished.

IN THE FEW SECONDS it took Gabe to get his bearings and approach the bar, Josie had already asked her question.

"I must know a ton of guys named Joe," the bartender said. "Probably seventy-percent are dark-haired and short. My sixteen-year-old grandson's the only one who comes to mind at this moment."

"My Joe would have already been an adult twenty-seven years ago," Josie said. "Is there anyone connected to Mary's who might recall something from that far back?"

"The owner had Mary's for three years, and he moved here from Des Moines." The barkeep eyed Josie. "I never met the old owners. I can't help you, sweetie, but good luck."

Josie shrugged at Gabe. "Guess I'll drive you home now."

"Sorry, kid."

They headed for the door.

"You asked about a *customer* before," said the old guy who'd been sitting at the bar.

Josie spun around. "What'd you say, Earl?"

"Coulda been Handsome Joe," the man said.

Josie returned to stand next to him. "Handsome Joe?"

"Yep." Earl slurped his drink. "Smallish fella. Tended bar here for a while."

"This Handsome Joe worked here?" Josie asked, her hazel eyes gigantic as she claimed the stool next to Earl.

Earl nodded. "He could mix up a good martini."

"Was this Handsome Joe a handyman?"

"Don't know 'bout that." Earl studied her out of the corners of his eyes. "Don't know much, in fact. You're not looking for money, are you?"

"Oh, no." Josie leaned her head nearer to Earl's and murmured, "This man could be my…uh. Well, he could be a relative. I want to talk to him, that's all."

Earl's shaggy brows lowered. "Could be the man had reason to stay away from the family. Ever think of that?"

Although Gabe had cautioned the same thing, he didn't like seeing the stab of pain in Josie's eyes.

But she acted okay. "I have," she said. "And I'm aware that this Joe might not even be the right one. But he could be. I need to find out."

The television momentarily snagging his attention, Earl picked up his glass and sipped noisily. Then he turned enough to eye Gabe behind him and Josie. "Short man. Black hair. Made a decent martini. That's all I know."

"Thanks so much. You did a good thing tonight." Josie swung off the bar stool and turned to give Gabe one of her "ready-to-go" faces.

Halfway to the door, however, Gabe glanced back at the clock.

Earl had swiveled clear around on the bar stool and was staring at Gabe.

He had more to say. Gabe just knew it.

Josie had grabbed her coat and disappeared outside. He wondered if she'd race off, only remembering later that he'd been with her. He could catch up to her, telling her to hold up. That Earl had something else to say.

The old man's stare summoned.

Gabe returned the stool Josie had just vacated. "You know something else, don't you?"

Earl sipped his drink and acted bored.

"If you do, say it. If not, I'm gone."

"Wasn't sure at first," the man rasped, "but after taking another gander at your girlfriend there, I am. Joe was the son of a couple who owned the hotel back in those days. Word was the family didn't have much to do with him. I figured everyone knew that. Everyone knows the Henshaws."

Earl squinted at Gabe, as if to make his meaning clear.

He figured *Gabe* knew that.

Joe *Henshaw.*

Oh, hell.

Now Gabe understood why his mother had been careful to avoid names. It made sense. His mom had a long time connection with the Henshaw family.

Alana Morgan had been Alana Henshaw before her divorce. She was Gabe's mother's friend, and she must be Joe's mother.

She could be Josie's grandmother.

Her son, whom Gabe remembered now as a Joe, had been estranged from the family for years. He'd been an alcoholic. He hadn't kept jobs. If the stories were true, he'd gotten messed up on drugs.

No wonder Gabe's mother had omitted details. She saw Alana regularly. They belonged to a few of the same clubs.

Alana had remarried several years ago, and she'd since been widowed. She never talked much about her youngest son. She talked about her daughter and her other son, both successful people who'd married and moved away.

Joe could still be living in Augusta.

He could become a real problem for Josie. He might ask her for booze or drug money. Or steal it. He might make Josie feel worse about her genetic makeup than she already did. How many times had Josie told Gabe she'd never marry because she feared that she'd inherit her mother's emotional problems?

Now she would learn that her father was the low-life bum her mother had described.

Damn it.

Gabe wished he could go outside and get into Josie's truck, refusing to tell her about this. If no one told her that Handsome Joe's last name was Henshaw, she might eventually abandon her search and settle into her life.

And if she discovered that Gabe knew the name, knew the blasted family…

She'd learned plenty on her own. If she kept asking around, she was bound to find her father. Gabe's only recourse was to help her and then be an ear for her.

Moments later, Gabe found Josie shivering in her truck, even though she'd started it and had the heater cranked all the way up. "Haven't you had your heater checked yet?" Gabe asked as he slid into the passenger seat.

"No."

The thing was blowing freezing air. "Why not?"

"Hello? I haven't had time?"

She usually wasn't so snippy. This search was taking its toll. "Make time," he said, but he doubted that she'd heard him because she was tearing out of the lot. He raised his voice. "Fix the heater, kid."

She laughed. "Tell me when, Gabe. I've had family at the house, and now I'm playing catch-up at work."

Gabe braced himself as she turned out onto Ohio Street and headed north, toward his house. He remembered the seat belt, buckled himself in and said, "Better watch for cops. They patrol near Mary's at this time of night."

"What took you so long in there, anyway?"

Although Gabe had decided he wouldn't avoid this confession, he'd hoped he could wait until they were inside one of their nicely heated houses.

"I thought you were right behind me," she continued. "But when I got outside, no Gabe! Did you decide to wait until I had the truck warmed up?"

He winced when she ran a very yellow light. "Maybe you'd better stop while I tell you about it."

"What? And sit at the side of the road, freezing to death? I'm wearing a skirt."

"Josie."

She noted his expression and quieted instantly.

After she'd pulled into the drive of an abandoned dry-cleaning shop, Josie shoved her gearshift into park but left the motor running. She waited quietly, as if sensing the importance of this moment.

"I got a name," he said.

Those eyes grew huge. "How?"

"When we were leaving, I noticed Earl watching me. I went back to talk to him."

"What did he tell you?"

"Handsome Joe's last name."

Josie looked as if curiosity might bust her eyes right out of her head.

"Henshaw. The name's Joe Henshaw. His family once owned the hotel on fifty-four."

Gabe wouldn't tell her the personal side of the story. That his mother knew Joe's mother. That they saw each other socially. That Josie had met the woman several times.

For one thing, Josie might press Alana for her son's address. Then Alana would wonder why she was looking for her son. What if his mom's friend didn't know about her son's association with Ella Blume?

Was it Gabe's place to expose this longtime secret? It sounded like a colossal mess. And he couldn't think of a way to explain his involvement, or lack of it, to anyone.

"Isn't that family still in town?" Josie asked. "If I remember right, the wife had her hand in all kinds of charity work."

"The Henshaws divorced," Gabe said. "The family might have scattered."

They had and Gabe knew it.

But Alana still lived here in Augusta. Gabe didn't know Joe's whereabouts.

He heard a shuffle and a click, then light flooded the cab of Josie's truck. She'd opened her door. "What are you doing, kid?"

"You'll see."

She ran around to her truck box and opened it to pull something out. When she crawled into the driver's side, she plopped a big phone book on the console between them and started thumbing through. "H-A. H-E. Here it is! Joseph A. Henshaw!"

Gabe peered at the address.

"Brookside Circle," she said, her voice husky with excitement. "Isn't that east of town?"

If Gabe placed it right, the address was in a small neighborhood off to itself. He'd driven through there once, exploring. He remembered tiny row houses, stray animals and overfilled trash bins. Signs of poverty.

"It's late, Josie. We can't go tonight."

"We can drive by," she said. "I think that address is off the old highway. We won't knock or anything, but I want to see his house."

If Gabe refused, she'd drop him off at home and go anyway. His efforts to caution her had been wasted.

"Okay, then. Let's go."

She put her truck into drive. "You sure you don't want me to take you home first?"

"No."

"What's your problem, then? I hear the reluctance in your voice." She veered out of the lot and toward the highway.

"You're jumping in with your eyes closed again, that's all," Gabe said. "Shouldn't you talk to your sisters before you pursue this?"

"He's not their dad," she said. "In my opinion, this evening couldn't have gone better. I have a name and address."

He bit his tongue. She'd heard his best arguments.

"I'm a big girl, Gabe."

He stayed quiet, watching her drive on.

Josie found the neighborhood easily. It wasn't as far into the countryside as Gabe had expected. Most of the houses were dark, but the lights of a television flickered behind the shaded windows of the listed address.

"I think this is it," she whispered as she pulled over to the curb.

The place was extremely small, and could have only three or four rooms, tops. Gabe couldn't see much in the darkness, just an impression of a shabby porch.

"Look, Gabe." Josie brushed a hand against his coat sleeve, then pointed.

"What is it?"

"Next to the door."

Someone had hung a wreath, beside the screen. Even in the darkness, the wreath looked lopsided. Cheap.

"Breaks my heart," she said. "He's welcomed Christmas."

Gabe knew then. This search wouldn't end tonight. He'd checked out that wreath and seen a bunch of gaudy plastic leaves. Josie had seen a holiday decoration. No matter what kind of a person she found inside, she would want to know him.

She sat there for moment, until Gabe finally suggested that she turn off the truck. No need to alert the neighborhood that someone was out here watching them.

She did, and seconds later a silhouette appeared in the front window. Josie gasped, but the shadow moved to the right until it disappeared. The occupant hadn't spotted them. Gabe guessed that the television was playing a commercial. He glanced at Josie and caught the new intensity in her posture.

"We can't go up there, Josie. It's well after eleven o'clock. Even if he's still dressed, he won't expect a visitor."

"I know."

"That might not even be the man."

She moved her focus from the distant door to Gabe, who was sitting in her line of vision.

"You don't even know for certain this is the house."

"Oh, but I feel it." She studied that porch again. "I think that man in there, who hung the wreath and watches television late at night, is my dad."

So did Gabe, and that worried him.

"You'll be okay, Josie. It doesn't matter who he is or what he's done with his life. You are you, no matter what you find out."

"Lord. Lighten up, Gabe." She sat gazing at the house, until the shadow reappeared briefly and then returned to the original spot. The commercials must have finished.

"Let's go before we freeze to death," Gabe said.

She didn't move.

"Josie! He might notice the truck and call the police."

Without speaking, Josie started the truck, circled around and headed west toward town. Obviously, she was full of her own thoughts.

"And don't show up here in the morning," he added. "Go to work. Come home. Let this settle."

"God, you're controlling. Just can it, won't you?"

Gabe clenched his jaw and shut up.

When Josie approached the main highway, Gabe expected her to whip onto the nearly empty thoroughfare, but she made a full stop at the street sign.

"I'm sorry," she murmured, glancing at him. "You've been great to help me through all this. I have no right to grouse."

"No problem, kid. I get that this is a big deal to you."

"You do, don't you?"

She continued toward home, again quiet. After she'd pulled into Gabe's drive, he entertained a wayward thought about asking her inside to pick up on their earlier kissing session. He couldn't fathom hopping out and jogging to the back door, as he had a hundred times before.

They'd gone beyond that, hadn't they?

But Josie had said it herself. She was distracted, confused. Busy. Her mind wasn't on him.

He reached for his door handle.

"Hey." She shifted the truck into park and turned in the seat, opening her arms to invite a hug. Her grin was remorseful, and she still looked a little lost.

He moved in her direction and found her easily in the small cab. Her warmth felt good in the still-frigid air.

Then Josie kissed him, her mouth firm if lingering. It was meant as a thank-you, Gabe was certain, but after a moment her lips softened and changed.

Their quick heat surprised Gabe, but he was willing. He kissed her back. Josie made a noise in her throat that sounded so feminine his body reacted with ready arousal.

Gabe moved his mouth deeper over hers, losing time

and all caution. Soon, he realized the cab was getting hot. *Really* hot. Josie's temperamental heater had kicked in, adding its blast to their inferno.

"Hot in here," he mumbled through the kisses. He wrestled out of his coat and helped her out of hers.

The material of her red jacket was thick. He wanted inside. He kissed for a while longer, then pushed a finger beneath a shiny black button and popped it open. He swooped down to inhale the wonderland of her cleavage, at the same time easing his hand beneath red lace to thumb her taut nipple.

She stilled.

She backed away to her side and faced forward.

"Josie?"

She shut off the heater and stared out the windshield for a moment, then looked at him. "What just happened?" she asked.

He took in her mussed hair. "I believe you gave me a thank-you kiss." He dropped his eyes, momentarily, to that single open jacket button.

She glanced down, swore and fastened it. "That was a kiss?"

"It started as one."

She shook her head, her eyes dark and miles wide. "We talked about this at Mary's, didn't we?"

"You said something about slowing down."

She waved at the air between them. "*This* was slowing down?"

He felt like a jerk. "I was letting you set the pace."

She let out a snort. "I think I meant stop."

"Josie? What's between us—it's…"

She shot out a palm, silencing him. "I can't, Gabe." She blinked at him a couple of times, then stared out the windshield again. "Not now, when so much else is happening. I can't do *us*. Can't you see that?"

Special, he'd been about to say. Instead, he waited until she faced in his direction again. "You're ending things now?" he asked.

"This isn't an ending," she insisted. "It's a…well… let's just keep things normal. Okay?"

"Normal?"

She nodded.

"Okay. Normal."

Gabe located his coat beside the seat, then gave Josie a quick salute before letting himself out of her truck. He did his best to jog to his back door, the same as he always did.

He spent most of that night convincing himself that she was right. Kisses could be forgiven. An intimate touch through fabric probably could, too. But indulging hotter, less-controlled desires would undoubtedly force choices that Josie wasn't equipped to handle right now.

Gabe had to remain strong.

And find *normal*.

Chapter Nine

Josie eyed her nephew, who stood near the chain-link fence of his yard, looking too sturdy and tall for his five years. "You ready?" she asked, and waited for his nod before she tossed the softball toward him in a slow, wide arc.

Luke swung and hit the ball easily, sending it flying into his mother's recently cleared pumpkin patch.

"Hey! You've been practicing!" Josie shouted as she chased the ball and avoided Luke's enthusiastic hustle from oak tree to garden edge to fence post.

When the little boy stepped across their Frisbee home plate, he hooted and she cheered. "Way to hustle, Lukey! You're some ball player!"

"I know." Luke's tone and expression held a hint of Callie's seriousness.

Josie laughed, enjoying that innocent confidence. With time and teaching he'd learn humility, but she liked him at this age, when he didn't realize he shouldn't broadcast his pleasure at his own success.

She pitched the ball to Luke a few more times, treasuring the gift of a sixty-degree December day. After two more solid hits into the garden, he knocked one into the neighbor's yard. "Oh, no!" he said, smacking his head.

"That's okay. Let's get the ball and then quit. Your parents should be home with Lilly any minute."

Luke tossed his bat into a large outdoor toy box, then grabbed her hand. Before they could head for the gate, however, Josie heard the clink of the gate opener.

Ethan walked into the yard, and Luke sailed across to meet him. As he swung the little boy up into his arms, Ethan said, "What have you been doing, sport?"

"Playin' ball," Luke said. "Is my sister okay?"

"She will be." He caught Josie's eye, including her in the conversation as he approached her. "Lilly responded well to an IV test for pyridoxine dependency—that's vitamin B6. We think we can eradicate her seizures by giving her megadoses of B6."

"That simply?" Josie asked.

"She's had the eye fluttering off and on, but they stopped after this morning's dosage. She's in the house now with Callie. Go look."

"Wow."

"I asked God to make my sister okay," Luke said, hugging his dad. "I'm glad He listened. She's a *cool* sister."

"We're glad, too," Josie said, winking at Luke.

Then she grinned at Ethan. "We need to get the softball from next door, then I'm going to talk to Cal a minute before I head to work."

"We'll get the ball," Ethan said. "Thanks for helping out. You're really returning to work? On a Friday after lunch?"

"I have a shipment of wallpaper and paint arriving at one of the houses. So yes, for as long as it takes to get that inside, I'm working. Then I'll take off for home."

Ethan put Luke on his shoulders and crossed to the gate. Josie went inside and found her sister in the hallway, folding the portable stroller. "You okay?" Josie asked.

"I'm so okay it's crazy." Callie set the stroller in her closet and turned to regard Josie. "I prayed this was something we could fix," she murmured. "And we're catching it early enough that she probably won't have any neurological damage."

"Probably?"

"Time will tell, but we have every reason to hope."

Callie and Josie peeked through the family-room door, where Lilly lay encircled by the several stuffed animals she'd received during her hospital stays.

She was so small and delicate. She hadn't learned to sit up yet, even at seven months, but she did appear awake and calm as she batted at a pink elephant.

"She looks good," Josie whispered.

"Doesn't she?" Callie beamed. "Thanks for watching Luke today, Josie."

"No problem. Just keep me in the loop, okay?" Josie returned to the hallway to pull her sweater from the closet. "I'm off to wait for some paint, then I'm going to do it."

Callie didn't have to ask what "it" was. "You're

visiting this Joe Henshaw?" she asked. "Didn't you just learn his name and address on Tuesday night?"

Josie looped her sweater over her arm and went to the door, where she stood with her hand on the knob. "I've had a hard time waiting this long. I've been swamped at work. Today's a lighter day, so I figured it was time."

"Be careful, hon. Are you taking Gabe along?"

Josie hadn't told Callie about Gabe. She couldn't confess that she'd asked him to back up, because only she and Gabe knew that she'd started anything.

Which was just the way she wanted it. Her sisters would tell her to grab on to Gabe and hang on tight. Izzy and Cal both loved him. The guys liked him, too. Their jaunt into forbidden territory would have to remain a secret. "Nope. Gabe's not going."

"Oh, honey, why?"

Because she was relying on him too much.

Kissing him too dang much.

And afraid of what that meant.

"He's swamped at work, too," she said.

And he hadn't called. Which wasn't exactly normal but probably for the best.

"Too bad," Callie said. "I don't like to think of you doing this alone. I want to hear about it afterward."

Josie went to the model home and discovered that her supplies hadn't arrived yet. She waited around for an hour, making a couple of phone calls to the delivery driver and studying her plans for each room.

The driver had been vague about his location. He could still be in Kansas City. If she received her things next Monday, she'd have wasted the afternoon.

She tried Gabe's cell number. She'd seen his car parked down the street when she'd driven past. He was helping a crew install a kitchen.

"H'lo."

"Yo, Gabe. It's me."

"Hi, kid. What're you doing?"

"Waiting for a paint delivery." She sighed, wishing she didn't have to ask Gabe for another favor. "I really need to leave for a while, though."

"Did you get hold of the driver?"

"Twice. He's on his way, he insisted."

Gabe was quiet, then said, "I can watch for the delivery. Where will you be if I have questions?"

"I'm going…home for a while," she said. "I'm not feeling well. Could be that virus that's going around."

"You're sick?"

"Might be."

"Are you making this up, Josie?"

Uh-oh. After mumbling some sound that could be a yes or no, she said goodbye and hung up. She locked the model home, thinking she might return later to check on the supplies. Maybe she'd even start the painting to give the crew a head start.

On her way past the house where Gabe was working, she glanced at the window and wondered if he was looking out.

After muttering an oath that would have infuriated her mother, Josie grabbed her phone from the dash and dialed Gabe's cell number again.

"H'lo."

"Me again."

"Hello, Josie."

"I'm not sick."

"I know."

"I'm going to see Joe Henshaw."

"I know."

"I'll tell you about it later."

She hadn't meant to fib, but Josie had no intention of contacting Gabe later. She could no longer drop by or telephone him three times a day.

He'd had his tongue in her mouth, and she his. He'd licked her between her breasts and she'd felt his body throbbing in preparation to enter hers.

How did two friends return to *normal* after that?

She was about to say goodbye and hang up, but Gabe interrupted. "Josie, let's do brunch tomorrow."

"Huh?"

"We need to talk more. Backing up isn't going to be all that easy. Everything between us…well, if we don't talk about how to handle it, it becomes more of an issue, doesn't it?"

Oh, boy. They had an *issue*. It sounded depressing. Josie avoided issues at all costs.

But he had a point. They couldn't exactly ignore what had happened. "Brunch. Okay. Where?"

He hesitated. "I want to say my place. We've eaten there together a thousand times and we've been fine. I believe we can handle it, don't you?"

She scowled into the phone. "Sure. In broad daylight, with the lights on and the windows and curtains open."

"Are you kidding?"

Not really. Thinking about him still got her hot.

She wouldn't say that to Gabe, though.

"Yeah, I'm kidding," she fibbed again. "We'll be fine at your place."

"Okay. Brunch, no sooner than eleven. That'll give us time to recover from whatever we do tonight."

That ending statement made Josie wonder about his plans for the night. Which weren't any of her business. Heck, the man should find some of those phone number slips and start dialing them.

They'd both be better off.

After driving to Augusta, Josie bypassed the turn to her house and continued east to Joe Henshaw's neighborhood. The area appeared different in daylight, but it was probably more frightening than it had been the other night. As she drove down the street, Josie noticed a general lack of upkeep. The people in this neighborhood must be too life-weary to care for their possessions.

And there sat Joe Henshaw's place, square in the middle of all the apathy. Was it less shabby than the rest of the dwellings, or was that only Josie's wishful thinking?

What was she getting herself into?

It didn't matter. She was going to do this, scared or not. She parked her truck at the curb and wished for the umpteenth time that she'd thought to phone first. But what did a person say in this situation?

Hi, this might be a surprise, but you slept with some woman a long time ago and conceived me.

At least Rick Blume had been married to her mother. This man may have never dreamed that he had a child, period.

Josie had just reached for her truck's door handle, when she saw Gabe's big car turn down the street.

She'd never been more glad to see that overpriced, ostentatious thing in her life. She scrambled out of her truck, then pretended a lack of concern when Gabe parked behind her.

"Thought you were going to watch for my paint delivery," she said as he approached her.

"I told my crew to keep an eye out for it."

She slid her truck key into a pocket and faced Gabe, wishing to God she could hit on that elusive normal. Teasing was her best bet. "Gabriel Thomas, contractor extraordinaire, left work when there was work to be done? I can't believe it."

He didn't smile. "You left work, too, Josie."

She held his gaze for a second, then dropped her eyes and touched the toe of his work boot with her sneaker. "I'm not renowned for being the most driven contractor in the area."

"No. But you are dedicated to your work. Usually."

Yeah. She'd been distracted lately. She glanced at the house—Joe's Henshaw's house—and forced herself to breathe evenly. "I appreciate your concern, Gabe. But I can manage this. You're supposed to back off, remember?"

"No, you asked for *normal*." Gabe waited until her eyes shot to his, then explained, "This is our normal. I'd have been here for you two years ago. I'm here now."

Josie nodded, then turned to stare at the house. She started toward it, knowing Gabe would follow.

"Did you call this time?" he asked as they climbed the steps.

"I did think about it," Josie whispered. "I wouldn't have had a clue what to say."

They stood side by side on the tiny porch, and Josie tried not to notice the dangling address number and the lopsided mailbox.

She hoped Joe Henshaw wasn't frail.

Could she handle her feelings if he was frail?

There was no doorbell. Her knock almost bounced the wreath off its nail and seemed to reverberate throughout the neighborhood. Josie imagined faces poking through every curtain and blind down the block.

She righted the wreath in the same moment that a man opened the door. He was only slightly taller than her and had thick salt-and-pepper hair. As he stood blinking at the brightness of a cloud-covered day, she noted eyes that were hazel and round, like hers, but bloodshot. Older.

She'd found her father.

The sounds of a televised football game drifted out from inside the house, and Josie stood there, with no idea how to start.

"Are you Joe Henshaw?" Gabe asked from beside her. Saving her butt, as usual.

"Ayuh."

An affirmative, Josie thought, although the man's voice had been gruff. His thick hair stuck out over his ears as though he hadn't combed it in a while. Had he been sick or did he always look this rumpled and tired?

"Well, if you're Joe Henshaw, then we're here to

see you," Gabe said, and stuck his hand out. "I'm Gabe Thomas."

"You came to see me?" Joe asked. He took a half step farther out, allowing the screen to rest against his back as the men exchanged a quick handshake.

Josie should introduce herself now. But how? She'd gone through this whole thing with Rick. She felt trapped in an endless circle of impossible situations.

I'm Josie Blume. Remember Ella? Surprise!

She cleared her throat. "Yes, um. Actually, *I'm* the one who's here to see you. Gabe's just…helping me." When she paused to catch her breath, she gazed down the street at all those front windows. "I'm wondering if you could invite us inside. Uh. The truth is, this is about your family."

Joe's eyebrows lowered over those intense hazel eyes. "I don't have family."

Oh, yes he did.

Josie had only met Joe. They'd exchanged the fewest of words. Yet she yearned to know him—this man with a short stature and big eyes and dark hair.

And she wanted him to know her, his daughter.

"I need to talk to you," Josie said. "I…I think this is something you'd like to hear. I promise, Gabe and I are safe."

Joe opened the screen door. "Come in, then."

He led them into a small room that reeked of cigarette smoke, then waved toward a stained green recliner that faced the television. The only seat in the room. "I have the one chair," he said. "You're welcome to it."

Gabe indicated with a nod that Josie should take the

chair, and after she did, he sat on the arm. Joe disappeared down a dark hallway and reappeared with a wood kitchen chair. She suspected that one was an only, too.

Joe leaned over the recliner, grabbing a pack of cigarettes from the table beside it. Then he positioned the other chair beside the doorway and sat down. He didn't pull out a cigarette and light it, thank God—it was already stifling in the tiny house—but he toyed with the pack. He tapped its end. He plucked out a cigarette and shoved it back inside. Josie suspected he was having a nicotine fit of monumental proportions.

She didn't hesitate any longer. "I'm Josie Blume."

The old guy frowned, finally tapping a cigarette all the way out of the pack and holding it between his fingers.

He didn't light it, though.

"I believe you knew Ella Blume, my mother?"

He rolled the cigarette between his thumb and index finger. Then he said, "Ayuh. 'Cept I wouldn't say I knew her. I knew *of* her."

He glanced at Gabe, who must have made some movement or expression that suggested doubt. Slight creases formed beside Joe's mouth—was that a grin?—then he muttered, "Mostly."

"Do you have any idea who I am, Joe?"

"I have suspicions."

"You slept with Ella Blume?"

He lifted his chin. "Once or twice."

"My mother had a baby from that once or twice."

Joe's mouth pinched into a tight line, then he harrumphed a sound of resignation. "I wondered," he said. "Can't say I'm shocked."

He stared at Josie, those eyes so round and bloodshot it hurt to look at them. She saw pain in his expression. She saw plenty of regret; that'd been there from the first minute.

And…interest?

She *wanted* to see interest. She wanted Joe to feel the same need for connection that she did.

But then he closed his eyes to speak, as if he couldn't deal with seeing Josie while speaking of the circumstances surrounding her conception. "Ella Blume never noticed me before that day. In her eyes, I was just some screw-up handyman, I could tell."

He harrumphed again, then coughed. That cough turned into a series that scared Josie, and when he finally caught his breath, he looked at Gabe again. "That day she was different. Looked at me as if she liked what she saw."

Joe returned his gaze to her. "But she never told me about you. When she had another baby, I had questions. She never spoke to me after that day, and I suppose I let myself assume a few things." He went into another fit of coughs.

Josie came half out of her seat to help him, but then he calmed and peered at her. "I don't know why you came here, girl." He lifted a pair of stocky, work-worn palms and glanced around the room. "If you need something, you see I have very little."

She glanced behind her at Gabe, wondering if he was catching all the similarities. The physical things—eyes, build. Joe's directness. He even lived alone.

Gabe gave her a wink, and she was glad, again, that he'd come. She might not feel the same courage without him.

"I didn't come to ask for anything," she said to Joe. "Only this—I recently discovered that I wasn't Rick Blume's daughter. I felt that I had to meet you."

He nodded, and the moment grew long.

Then Joe chortled, a loud, rattling noise that went on and on and seemed to surprise him. "Guess Ella got the last laugh on the whole town for yakking around about her," he finally said.

Josie snickered. "She was sly, that's for sure."

Joe's chuckles turning to coughs, and his thick chest heaved so deeply he bent forward in the chair. When he calmed, those hollows beneath his eyes appeared to have deepened. He blinked, as if very tired. Confused.

And done.

Josie glanced backward at Gabe, and he gave her a nod and slid off the arm of the chair.

"We should go," he said as he and Josie stood together in that tiny living room. "Josie would like to contact you again. You okay with that?"

Did Joe's face soften as he faced her? Did his eyes brighten by some minuscule degree? "Can't hurt to talk," he said, and gifted her with the faintest grin that charmed her completely.

"It can't hurt," she repeated.

"Okay." Joe walked them the three paces to the door, still fondling that dang cigarette.

After a goodbye, Gabe guided Josie out, down the steps and across the lawn. When she turned to look,

Joe's door was closed. Once more, the wreath had gone crooked.

"You handled that well," Gabe said when they reached her truck.

She located her key and opened the driver's side door, then stood just inside it while Gabe paused on the grass next to the vehicles. "Thanks. I was scared out of my gourd."

"You headed home?"

"God, yes. I'm set on some recuperation time. I'll catch up with work next week. Surely that paint will arrive by Monday morning."

"I can call the crew and ask about that delivery."

"That'd be great."

"Okay, then," he said.

Josie thought he'd leave, but he didn't. After a couple of beats, he asked. "Want company? Now, I mean?"

God, yes.

But then Gabe might decide they should talk about things now, and it was all so strange. She felt wired. Weird. She didn't feel strong in her resistance.

The opposite, in fact. She looked at Gabe and wished he didn't mean so much to her.

"We'd better not, Gabe."

"Not even if it's normal for us?"

"Not even."

"You're still happy with this choice, Josie? This is what you want?" He spoke the words softly, personally, as if he was physically closer to her than he really was.

"Yes. I'm happy with it. And you get on with things, okay? Find one of those paper scraps. Call some woman and go out *tonight.* Forget this idea of you and me. I just…don't…have it in me."

He turned to start for his car. Looked back. "I had to try."

"I know."

Chapter Ten

"That one's a hunk, Josie. See if you can get him to buy you a drink."

Moving her gaze to the man whose attention her table mate had just drawn with her giggled comment, Josie nodded at the handsome stranger two tables down, then averted her gaze.

The man was too old. Too conservative. Too handsome in a blond, all-American, Gabriel-Thomas way.

Instead of returning to her work site or sitting home in a tizzy tonight, Josie had summoned the chutzpah to come to Mary's alone. She'd figured she could hook up with some of her female acquaintances.

Which she had.

She shouldn't be in a blue mood at all. She'd found her dad this afternoon, and in doing so had met a goal. She'd learned that she was shorter and darker than her sisters because she took after her father. She had reason to believe she'd learn a lot of other things in the future.

But she had to survive tonight first.

She didn't want to be here at Mary's. She hadn't

wanted to stay at home. This thing with Gabe confused her, and she couldn't talk about it because no one knew except Gabe and her.

She knew she'd been right to stop that mess.

A wham-bam thing would never work between her and Gabe. They knew each other too well. That left commitment, and she'd never been the type to hang on after the fun of newness wore off.

What's more, now she had evidence that her mother's questionable mental health was only half of an unlucky gene pool. Her father had some nasty habits.

God. No wonder she preferred beer and parties to cola and books. She took after her dad.

So she'd come out alone tonight. She'd arrived at Mary's a little late, approached these women she saw here often, and asked if she could join them. She was in the mood to party hard and long, she'd claimed.

They'd introduced themselves again, but Josie had already forgotten most of the names. The redhead was Kendra. That name had stuck because the tall dental assistant had gone out with Gabe a time or two.

Now Josie sat with a soft drink, analyzing the crop of guys and hoping that something—*anything*—would happen to snag her notice and make the night pass.

Anything except that.

Gabe had just walked in with a honey-eyed blonde. How could Josie miss them? The woman wore sparkles. Purple, shimmering dress, jewel-bedecked hair. And Gabe was sublime in his olive Corbin suit. They must be on their way to or from somewhere classier than Mary's.

Within seconds, Kendra, too, had spotted them. "Josie, isn't that your Gabe?"

"He's not *my* Gabe," Josie corrected her. She hunched down on her seat, but she recognized that her effort to hide was futile. Mary's wasn't nearly crowded enough.

"Hey, Gabe!" Kendra hollered, waving wildly. "Josie's over here."

Oh, crud.

She should have warned these gals that she was avoiding him. She'd never have thought he'd show up with a woman tonight, even if she'd suggested it.

As Gabe and the blonde approached the table, he held Josie's gaze until he stood in front of her. "I didn't except to see you here tonight," he said after he'd stopped across from her.

"I didn't know I'd see you, either," she countered.

Sparkles moved closer to him.

Gabe faced the group of women. "You haven't met Shelby, ladies. Shelby Roberts, this is, uh…" He paused as he studied the brunette in the far left seat.

Josie stifled a laugh. If she couldn't remember her table mates' names, Gabe certainly couldn't.

"Well, the woman in blue there is DeeAnn. Then there's Kendra and next to her is D.W. Josie's the one at the wall. She's the one I told you about."

None of the woman corrected him. He must have paid more attention to names than she had. Perhaps he'd dated each of them, at various times.

The thought was stupid.

Besides Kendra, he hadn't gone out with any of

them. The two Dees were too old for him, and one of them wore a wedding band. It shouldn't matter if he'd dated every woman in the group at once.

Apparently, he and this Shelby were on a date now.

Josie should be glad. She had no reason to detest the woman on sight.

"Would you care to join us?" Kendra asked.

The other ladies hopped off their stools and scooted them nearer to Josie, who was already crammed in next to the wall.

She stared at her soft drink and refused to look at Gabe. She wouldn't give him permission to join them, silently or otherwise. After abandoning her efforts to transform her 7Up into the beer she'd thirsted for anyway, Josie looked up to see that Gabe had borrowed two chairs from a nearby table. He and the sparkly Shelby sat shoulder-to-shoulder next to the aisle.

"Thanks for the invitation," Shelby said. "Gabe really bailed me out tonight and escorted me to my cousin's holiday party. I hate going to those things alone, especially when everyone else is coupled up." She lowered her voice and leaned forward. "My cousin thinks I'm an old maid, and I'm only twenty-nine! Can you believe it?"

Okay, so Shelby was not only tall and blond, like all Gabe's dates, she was also nice. Like all his dates.

He definitely had a type, and it wasn't short-haired, short-legged brunette party girls.

Aw, jeez. *This* was not thinking about him?

When the waitress arrived to get Gabe's and Shelby's orders, Josie asked her to take the 7Up and return with a beer. Then she listened to the conversation about Shelby's cousin's dinner.

She surveyed the bar, too. When she saw a curly-headed guy standing with his back to her, she kept her eye on him. Perhaps the rest of him was as cute as his butt.

Gabe had brought a date here. Maybe she could take one home.

Josie heard Shelby say her name, and focused on the conversation she hadn't quite been able to tune out. "And I'm so glad he invited me here now," Shelby was saying. "He told me about your day, Josie. Must have been tough."

The waitress brought their orders before Josie had had time to bark out a laugh or a question or an objection.

But her face must have registered surprise.

"Meeting your father that way is what I meant," Shelby said.

Gabe had told this…this *stranger?* About a day she'd never forget? It was no big secret, but it was her business.

She glanced at Gabe, then away.

She was tempted to ask Shelby if he'd kissed her with tongue yet, so they could compare notes. Instead, she faked cool. "My day was fine," she said. "Excuse me, ladies. I see someone I know."

Everyone at the table stood up or scooted forward or sideways or however. Josie grabbed her beer and squeezed out. She made a beeline toward the pool room. She'd seen the curly-haired man go in there, but any man would do.

When she realized that her curly-haired man was actually the Juco student she'd met before Halloween, she felt a small disappointment.

She yanked on his sleeve anyway. "Wisconsin! That *is* you, isn't it?"

The guy turned to eye her. "Huh?"

"Wanna dance?"

He scowled. "Don't you have a boyfriend?"

"No, I do not. Mind if I put my beer on your table?"

"You don't?" He eyed her warily, then shrugged. "This isn't my table. Uh…" He scrunched up his brow, as if trying to figure out if he'd answered all her questions.

"We dancing?" she repeated.

"Uh…okay."

Josie set her bottle on the empty table and attached her palm to the middle of Wisconsin's chest. He was promoting the Georgia Bulldogs tonight. After gathering the sweatshirt material into her fist, she pulled him toward the tiny area near the deejay station, where couples occasionally danced.

In her rush to leave the table, Josie had forgotten to grab her keys. She couldn't leave Mary's. She couldn't return to the table and admit she'd run off in a huff because of Gabe's big mouth.

As she danced a two-step with Wisconsin, Josie flirted outrageously—something she hadn't done in ages. She was using the poor guy and she felt badly about that, but Gabe could be watching her.

The Juco student asked twice more if she had a boyfriend, and she assured him that she was completely unencumbered. His expression registered doubt until a slow song started and Josie kept dancing with him.

A moment later, Gabe and Shelby came out to the dance floor, too.

Josie could leave now. She could go to the table, grab her keys and head home.

But if Gabe noticed that she'd left soon after his arrival, he might wonder if his presence had affected her.

Which it had.

She'd never admit that to him.

So she stayed out there for a second song. Wisconsin grew so confident he thought he could explore her derriere with his hands. Josie promptly moved them to a more appropriate place, but made sure to chuckle about it.

And when he tried to kiss her neck, she pulled his chin up and gave him a stern look. "No kissing on the first slow dance set," she said. "I'm not that kind of girl."

"But you are crazy," he said, grinning widely. "What's your name?"

She slid a glance past his shoulder and wished she hadn't. Shelby had her eyes closed.

"Sarah," Josie half fibbed.

"You live here in Augusta, Sarah?"

"I live up in Woodbine," she lied again.

And promised herself she'd behave for two weeks. No beer, even at home on weekends.

"Can we get together?" Wisconsin asked. "Maybe we could meet here sometime when it isn't so crowded." He leaned back to study her. "Or we could go out somewhere. Your call."

"I don't know," Josie said. "I don't get down to Augusta often. Really."

Okay. She wouldn't eat chocolate for those two weeks she was off beer and on good behavior, and she'd write personal letters to put in her Christmas cards. Heck. She'd send the Christmas cards out before Valentine's day this year.

"You were here before though, right? With a boyfriend?" Wisconsin peered toward Gabe, then shook his head. "That was you, right?"

"Could have been my sister. Er…Sadie. She and I are practically twins. She comes down here, too. Just…not at the same time I do."

So she'd shop for Christmas presents early, try to beat all her work deadlines and eat nothing but fruits, veggies and fish for two weeks.

Three.

And she would never lie to this poor kid again.

"Are you lying to me?" A corner of Wisconsin's mouth turned up, as if he was proud of himself for catching on.

"Maybe." She sighed. "Yes. I just needed a guy to dance with really quick. I had no time to investigate whom I was grabbing. Listen, if you find yourself in a pinch, I'm your gal, okay?"

Wisconsin nodded. "I get it."

"You get what?"

"That tall guy with the blond babe broke your heart, so now you're trying to make him jealous."

Well, not exactly. But almost.

"Want me to help you make the show really good?" Wisconsin dropped his gaze to her lips. "We could kiss. I'd act as though I was really into it. We could even leave together."

Even if Josie had been tempted, she'd gotten herself into trouble kissing a man she shouldn't. She wouldn't repeat that mistake tonight. It was time for this game to end. "Wisconsin, you're not a bad guy, if a little too fast. You should spend time with that beautiful kid of yours."

"You've seen my little boy?"

"No, I haven't. But he's a child and he's yours. If he's not beautiful to you, then you don't know him."

"Oh."

"That's my biggest rule. I don't go out with guys who abandon their children." She lowered her voice. "It's a personal thing with me."

"Okay."

"Thank you for the offer. I'm leaving alone."

Now that she'd said the words, Josie realized she could do so. Gabe and his date were on the dance floor. An acceptable period of time had passed. She could grab her keys and escape. "See you around," she told Wisconsin, standing on tiptoe to peck him on the cheek.

Josie started toward the table, which had been abandoned except for the collection of drinks, change and keys. The other women must have made a restroom trip. She should be able to sneak out.

Avoiding the briefest glance at the dance floor, she sat down long enough to summon the waitress and pay her bill. But when she grabbed her keys and got up to leave, Kendra appeared in front of her, blocking her way.

"Josie, where you going?" she asked. "Gabe ordered a round of drinks. The bottle at your spot is full."

"You drink it," Josie said, pushing it over. "I'm giving up beer for a couple of weeks. Good night."

Now Gabe approached the table. "You're leaving?" He checked his watch. "But it's ten-fifteen."

"My God! It's past ten? No wonder I'm so exhausted."

Shelby appeared behind him, possessively laying a hand on his bicep. Then the other women, all taller than Josie, crowded around to ask what was happening.

"Josie's leaving," Kendra murmured.

"I thought she said she was in the mood to party all night?" someone said.

Josie felt trapped by the well-intentioned acquaintances surrounding her. She searched for an escape.

"She did say she was here to party. Something must have happened," someone else whispered, way too loudly.

"Was that Georgia guy mean to her?"

"I don't know, but I think she and Gabe are mad at each other."

Josie couldn't tell who had made the last comment, but it was enough. She poked the set of ribs in front of her, causing that person to squeal and jump backward.

After darting through the opening, she left the bar. She didn't realize Gabe had followed her until she was in the lot.

"Josie."

She rolled her eyes and spun around, walking backward. "Go inside, Gabe. Find your date."

"I wanted to be sure I didn't upset you," he said. "I had no idea you'd be here."

She stopped at her truck, which was parked near the front door of the bar. No way he could have passed it without noticing it. "Uh-huh."

She stuck her key in the lock.

"After I drove into the lot, I saw your truck, of course. But by then I'd already told Shelby I was taking her in for a drink."

"Right." Josie opened her door, then hesitated. "Hey, Gabe. I can't do the brunch after all."

"What?" By now he was very near. She could feel his breath, hot on her cheek.

"I can't do it," she repeated. "I have plans. I'll be busy all day tomorrow. Sorry."

"Josie."

She got in, closed the door and started the truck. Without waiting to put on her seat belt or turn on her headlights, she tore out of the lot.

By the time she'd approached Ohio Street, she'd settled herself enough to drive home safe.

Emotionally, she was a wreck. She was embarrassed, and she felt chicken. She hated that.

Saying or hearing any of the words that would have been spoken at brunch would have hurt like hell, so why exchange them? They both must wish the words weren't necessary.

Josie hated the way she'd behaved around Gabe

tonight, but normal seemed like some distant memory. So she would avoid the conversation—avoid Gabe— until something else happened or she figured out how to contain her raging emotions.

And now she'd have to find something to do all day tomorrow, in case Gabe called or came by the house to check on her. He must have done that a hundred times after a night out at Mary's.

Josie couldn't even hide the truck and hole up in the house. The dang key trade.

She'd get her set back as soon as possible. Not normal, perhaps, but necessary until she'd recuperated enough to handle the tumult her life had become.

A FEW DAYS LATER, Josie sat watching Joe toy with his cigarette pack. He was in his recliner—she'd taken the kitchen chair this time—and had to be wishing she would leave so he could light up.

At least he'd known she was coming tonight. She'd called him on Sunday evening, asking if there was a good time for a visit this week. Sometime after work. That was when she'd learned that he currently worked an overnight shift at a printing business here in town. She'd have to visit late in the evening, when he was awake and preparing for work.

Josie had arrived about an hour ago, and she felt they were hitting it off rather well.

"So you're the black sheep of the family?" Joe asked her, responding to her comment that Ella had always compared her with her sisters.

"I wouldn't say that," she said. "Mother tried to tame

my bad habits, but she also told me she was proud of me fairly often."

"I wasn't the black sheep either," he said. "People talk about their black sheep, if only to complain about the trouble they cause. I'd say I'm the family's five-legged sheep."

"Five-legged?"

"The one that's sort of strange, that no one in the family talks about?"

Josie laughed with him, then shook her head. "Your family's around, then?"

"Mother's still here in town."

"Do you visit her?"

"No. You been married, Josie?"

Smiling at the rapid change of subjects—one of her own avoidance techniques—Josie shook her head. "Nope."

"What? You don't like men?"

"I like them *too* much."

"What about the tall fellow you brought with you a few days ago?"

"Gabe's a friend," Josie said. "And please don't pair us up, even in your thoughts. I noticed *you* aren't married."

"Too many bad habits. I'm not marriage material."

How many times had Josie said that marriage made people fat and boring, that she wanted nothing to do with it?

Joe fussed with his cigarette pack. Josie had reasons to believe that he drank, too. She'd seen several liquor bottles on his countertop a while ago, when she'd gone in to get the kitchen chair.

All those years that her mother had talked about alcoholic men, she must have been talking about Joe.

Who'd have suspected?

"I have my own vices," Josie said. "Or Mother would say so. I like noise. Beer. Parties."

Joe lifted out of his chair. "Did I offer you something, girl? I can't drink just before work, but I'm sure I've got something in the fridge."

"You did offer. Sit down. I have to work tomorrow."

"Your drinking's not a vice, then." He eyed his cigarettes. "You don't smoke?"

"No."

"Then you're fine, girl. You're honest. You work hard. You're beautiful."

She must have looked doubtful.

"You're thinking you're not?" her father said. "But you have clear skin, a straight nose and big, sparkly eyes. You carry yourself as if you're happy. You must catch the eyes of men everywhere you go."

Josie beamed at him, happy in a moment every daughter should experience at least once: hearing that her father considered her attractive and why. The memory must carry over through a girl's entire life.

"Actually, you remind me of my sister," Joe added.

"I do?"

"Oh, yeah. She was hot stuff—a cheerleader in high school. She won one of those titles—prom princess? She has that same rounded face with big eyes. Hers are blue, though. The guys were gaga over her when she was single."

"I get along with guys," Josie said. "But mostly

because I don't spout my emotions all the time. I'm more of a tomboy."

"You don't date?"

"I do. And the guy and I talk about sports and cars. We have fun."

"They might keep seeing you because you're fun, but they ask you out because you're pretty."

Josie's "Thank you" was buried beneath another of Joe's coughing fits. These coughs were deep and angry. "You okay, Joe?" she asked when he calmed.

"I do this every winter." He coughed another couple of times. "Bronchitis probably."

"Have you consulted with a doctor?"

Josie eyed her as if she'd suggested that he yank out his own tonsils.

"You should see someone about your cough."

"Why? I smoke. I feel no need to have someone tell me it's bad for me. I'm aware that it is, but it's my choice."

She returned to her chair and debated whether to state the obvious. Since she was practical and plain-spoken, she did. "It could be something you could fix, though, Joe. You ought to check it out."

"Whatever it is, I don't need to know," he said. "If it's bad and I go, my absence will hardly be noticed."

Now, why did that statement hurt? Josie had just met the man.

"I like you, Josie-girl, but I don't need any more family coming around to tell me how to handle myself. I'm a stubborn old cuss who's chosen a life that suits me."

Josie realized then that Joe was smart. This is who

I am, he was saying. Right off. Allowing her the choice to proceed with caution or retreat.

Her earlier analysis had been wrong.

Joe wasn't some weak-minded guy her mother had found for her specific purpose. He was more than that. Perhaps Ella had held some small, private affection for him.

The thought was surprisingly comforting.

Joe recognized what he'd sacrificed because of his bad habits. He might be a fool, but he wasn't a blind fool.

"Have you told your mother about me?" Josie asked.

"Nope. As I said, I don't talk to her."

Anything else Joe might have said was taken over by a new round of coughs. When he finally quieted, he said, "Listen, I had a good time tonight, but I should get ready for work." He eyed that pack of cigarettes as if he was growing desperate for them.

She stood and grabbed her coat from the chair back. Her father had given her a good hour. She was satisfied.

"Could you stand another visit, maybe this weekend?" she asked as she buttoned her coat.

He led her to the door. "I'd like that."

Josie hugged him very gently, noticing not the frailty of his bones, as she had with Rick Blume, but the warm strength of his hold on her.

As she drove home, Josie chuckled a few times, remembering snippets of conversation. When she'd first asked Joe for this visit, she'd done so partly as an excuse to get out of the house. Because of the Gabe situation. He'd been calling her, trying to set up another time for that talk. She'd managed to avoid him.

But when Josie turned down her street, she saw Gabe's car parked in her driveway.

She was tempted to leave again. Perhaps she could visit Callie and Ethan and avoid home for another few hours. At that moment, however, she'd rather face Gabe. She hoped to tell him about her evening with Joe.

She'd missed Gabe. Now that she was over her jealous funk about Shelby, perhaps she could handle a return to friendship.

Except…*crud!* How could she explain her behavior the other night? Gabe would surely have recognized her silly antics for what they were: out-of-control emotions. She'd acted…girly.

She could admit that it had hurt to know that he'd confided her private situation to his date.

That was a girly response, too, but it was the easiest truth to tell. She'd use that one, see what Gabe said, then let him know that she was fine—herself again, and not thinking about him all the time.

Gabe's friendship was surely worth another fib.

Chapter Eleven

Gabe was in Josie's kitchen when he heard her walk in. After days of trying to catch her, he'd finally decided to bring some clothes and stay until she came home for a change of hers.

It was time to lay this attraction problem out between them and deal with it. He wasn't ready to chuck the relationship forever. He loved that little gal as much as he loved his own family, but in an oddly more personal way—as if her happiness was somehow his responsibility.

Josie walked straight into the kitchen, took off her coat and draped it over a chair. She tossed her keys onto the counter opposite him, then leaned against it to eye him.

Gabe realized he was jumpy. If he said something wrong, he could scare Josie away again. He longed to do the opposite. He lifted his palm and tried a simple "Hello."

She snickered. "This is tough, isn't it?"

"Oh, yeah."

"Well, let's make it easier," Josie said. "I'll admit that I was in a snit for a while. I'm over it."

"A snit? Because of Shelby?"

"Because it wasn't your place to share my personal news with a stranger."

"Personal news?"

"That I'd met my father for the first time."

He'd hoped Josie was jealous. Wonderfully, charmingly jealous. He still thought she might have been, even if she didn't admit it.

"Shelby made it sound as if I'd poured my heart out about you and Joe, but it wasn't that way at all."

Josie took off her coat and dropped it over the back of a chair. "How was it, then?"

"Friday night was our first date and it was hardly a date," Gabe said. "Shelby had asked me to go to this dinner several times, and I finally gave in about an hour beforehand. I forgot about the talking problem."

"What talking problem?"

"Shelby's. She babbles."

"Oh."

"So by the time we were getting in my car to head to the cousin's house, I'd already listened to about twenty minutes of chatter. When she asked about my day I was relieved." He shrugged. "I told her about it."

Josie snorted.

"Besides, I've always talked to the women I date about you. I don't remember you being angry about it."

She pinched her lips together.

Okay. Things had changed. If Josie didn't want to believe it, he did. Gabe figured that their relationship had started shifting sometime after Halloween.

They'd kissed, and for the first time acknowledged

the sexual energy between them. Or maybe it'd been before Halloween, whenever he'd started feeling jealous of the men who flirted with Josie.

That was what he wanted to talk to her about tonight. Maybe they could stop the touching and kissing, but how would they handle the out-of-place feelings?

"I screwed up, telling Shelby," he said. "It was an old habit. I apologize."

"Forget it. I'm fine." She rolled her eyes and let out a huffy sigh. "But, Gabe? I'm not comfortable with this key trade idea, anymore."

"Key trade?"

"You're in my house. You let yourself in."

"Uh-huh."

"I think you should wait for an invitation now, okay? Still friends, but more respectful of privacy."

Yeah. He had felt odd letting himself in today. "Sounds fair."

"I'll give you your keys. You return mine." She grabbed her key ring and wrestled with it. He pulled his set from his pocket and detached her house and truck keys. After a moment, they met in the middle of the kitchen and traded.

"Oh! Your car key's on my dresser. I never got around to putting it on my ring. Be right back." She started down the hallway that led to her bedroom.

He couldn't follow her.

Even if he did tackle her on a run and bounce her onto her bed, Josie knew self-defense. She'd use it on him.

Probably.

She had kissed him back rather vigorously on several occasions. She'd allowed him to explore her bare skin once.

She'd played tongue tag with him.

Hell's bells. He couldn't go back to her bedroom.

Gabe leaned against Josie's kitchen counter, staring out the sliding-glass doors into the backyard and trying to think of something besides that hot jealousy in her eyes whenever he mentioned Shelby.

He wondered where she'd been these past few days. Out with Wisconsin, despite his single-dad status?

Gabe's intention to talk calmly about choices vanished. He wanted to ask if Josie had missed him as much as he'd missed her. Had she missed her old friend Gabe?

Or the man she'd been kissing?

He wanted sex and forgiveness and a mutual responsibility to protect each other's feelings—

Here she was.

She walked in and gave him his spare car key. As he took it from her, their knuckles touched. Gabe could imagine himself grabbing her wrist, yanking her forward and kissing her until she recognized the rare passion in his touch.

Until she felt it, too.

But Gabe lived with his feet on the ground.

And the moment moved away. "I told Shelby I wouldn't be seeing her anymore," he said.

"So soon?" Josie asked, her voice breezy as she stood beside him, next to the fridge.

"Nadine was sure I'd like her, too. I guess sisters aren't always the best matchmakers."

"Well, Shelby was nice." Josie sounded *too* cool. "And she was that tall blond type you go for."

Gabe was tempted to call Josie's bluff and kiss her. If she was bluffing.

She turned to yank open her refrigerator door to investigate the contents, as though bored with the subject.

If he'd found the courage, Gabe could have told her that he'd avoided the good-night kiss with Shelby, even though the teacher had hinted that she'd be receptive.

Instead, Gabe had told her he was uninterested, forever and always, and had hurried home to imagine hot, bathtub kisses with Josie.

Josie shut the fridge door after a moment, then moved across to the opposite counter. She didn't look prepared for a feelings conversation.

"You been out?" he asked.

"I visited Joe again."

She'd gone alone? "How did that go?"

"Better than you might think. He has some bad habits, but he was open with me. He's smart. Sincere. I think we're going to get along very well."

Gabe curbed a hug impulse. "I'm glad."

She began listing some of the things that Joe had done and said, and Gabe listened with a smile on his face. Other folks might have been put off by their discovery of a poor man who'd made irresponsible choices.

Josie would forgive the superficial things. She'd find the good in a person.

Lord, he loved that about her. Not just her pluck or her eyes or her laugh. He loved the way she viewed the world through kind eyes.

"He acted as though he enjoyed our conversation as much as I did," Josie said, her voice growing stronger as she got into the telling of her experience. "I see so much of myself in him, too."

Gabe fought to control his thoughts. "Like what?"

"He's also the youngest of three, and he claims that his brother and sister are perfect." She shook her head, laughing. "He jokes about it the same way I do."

"I happen to prefer you to your sisters. They are remarkable. But they aren't you."

The tinge to Josie's cheeks was all the thanks he needed.

"This has been surreal," she said. "At Halloween, I set out to find my father for Lilly's sake—Callie's and Isabel's and my father, that is. It's not even Christmas and I know I'm their half sister. And I've met my own dad."

Suddenly, she looked lost.

Damn it. This was a tough time for Josie. Could Gabe not remember that for ten minutes?

He sat at her kitchen table and used his foot to scoot a chair out across from him. "Get comfortable," he said. "Tell me more about this visit."

"Would you like a beer?" she asked, opening her refrigerator door again. "Dang. I only have one. It's yours if you want it."

"You go ahead."

She brought the beer to the table. Then she contemplated it for a moment and replaced it in the fridge. She crossed to the cupboard, grabbed two glasses and filled them with milk.

As she set one of them in front of him, Gabe stared at it. Then her. "Turning over a new leaf?"

She laughed as she sat down. "Just drink the dang milk."

He watched her, noticing the gloss of her very short, very dark hair and the way the style suited her small, pretty features.

When had he decided that Josie was beautiful?

"As I said before," Josie went on, "he was great."

She stopped herself. Took a drink of the milk and peered toward her back window. Her eyes showed a worry she hadn't voiced.

"There's a but after the end of that statement, isn't there?" he asked.

She lifted a shoulder. "He was coughing again, a lot this time, and his skin had a gray tone. I don't think he's healthy."

"He probably doesn't live very well."

"He practically issued a challenge to me, to proceed only if I'm willing to accept him the way he is."

"Sounds like something you'd do."

Her father was very lucky to have met Josie.

And Gabe knew he was head over heels. If he never found an opportunity to retool this friendship into a relationship, he'd die loving Josie and masquerading as her devoted friend.

It was time to change the subject.

"Josie."

Her expression was guarded, but she listened.

"I realize we've agreed. Friends and no more. Right?"

She nodded.

"I'm not sure we should curb the attraction."

A darkness fell over her face.

"Why avoid it?"

"Because if we try something more than friendship, we're essentially ending the friendship."

"Not necessarily."

"What are you suggesting?"

"Marriage?"

She looked confused.

"We feel that strongly about each other."

Josie scowled, as if thinking hard about his statement, then said, "I'm not sure about that. I love you. You know that. And I can't deny that I'm attracted...."

"But?"

"But I believe this is just temporary madness."

"Not for me."

"How can you be certain?" she asked. "I've needed you so much lately and you're flattered. Maybe you're confusing those feelings."

"No."

"Yes."

Gabe sighed. "So what do we do?"

She took her milk glass to the sink and ran water in it. "Maybe you should tell Shelby you made a mistake."

So Josie wasn't ready.

At least she wasn't running.

"Have it your way," he said. "But please stop dodging me. I want to see you."

"I think I can handle that."

"Good."

He kept looking at her back until she turned to meet his gaze, and he held it for a moment.

Saying more with his expression. Showing her that he was steady and all right and ready to hold strong as her friend for as long as necessary.

WHEN JOSIE HADN'T shown up at his house by two the very next Sunday, Gabe put away the extra sandwich and tried not to think about the empty recliner next to him. Although they'd never discussed their plans to spend big football Sundays together, they'd been doing so for well over two years now. Hell, he'd cut Saturday-night dates short so he could have the house ready for Josie's visits. He was fairly certain that Josie had done the same thing. It was tradition.

But today he'd had the food laid out, the drinks chilled and the game going, and she'd gone missing. She hadn't answered her phone a while ago, and the Chiefs were doing great. They were up by seven, two minutes from half-time.

She wasn't working. She'd finished the second model home on Friday, and she wouldn't start a new one on the weekend.

Her whereabouts were no mystery, however. The woman was obsessed.

Gabe devoured his sandwich, but realized he wasn't focusing on the game when the crowd roared. The Chiefs had scored, and he'd missed it. He was three feet from the blasted television.

At half-time, he hopped in his car and drove by Josie's house. She wasn't there, of course.

Her constant pop-in visits were probably driving the old man crazy. Joe refrained from smoking when his daughter was visiting, so he probably got pretty fidgety. Maybe Gabe should go by and rescue the pair from each other.

He circled Josie's block, then headed east to Joe Henshaw's place. It looked better already, Gabe realized as he drove up. Josie had cleared some sprouting trees from the side of the porch, replaced the bolt in the dangling mailbox and reaffixed the address letters. She must have been spending all her spare time here.

Good for her. Gabe wasn't surprised and he didn't blame her. He should go home and turn on the game again. Or he could drop by Mary's. Earl might be there, watching the Chiefs.

Or he could go in and say hi to Joe.

Before he could change his mind, Gabe parked and strode to the door to knock.

Josie answered, wearing the distracted look she got when she was busy. "Gabe?"

"I figured you were here."

At her questioning expression, he reminded her, "The game?"

"Aw, Gabe, I forgot." She hesitated, then pushed open the screen door. "Want to come in?"

"Sure."

She motioned him inside. "But be quiet," she murmured. "He's in bed. I'm going to leave in a minute and make a big grocery store run."

Josie was generally the "grab something when I need it" type. "You get tired of takeout?" he asked.

"My dad's the one who needs groceries."

As they entered the kitchen together, Gabe noticed that Josie had left the cabinet doors and drawers open. She'd dumped a bunch of boxes and bags into the trash can, and she had a shopping list started on the counter.

"Joe got up to let me in about an hour ago, but he looks awful," she said. "I insisted that he lie down again."

This was a leap. Less than two weeks ago, Josie and her dad were barely more than biologically tied strangers. Today she was acting as his caregiver.

"I intended to make him some soup for lunch, but I could only find liquor and stale food. Some of the cereal was moldy. Can you imagine? That stuff's full of preservatives."

He could imagine. Joe had lived his entire adult life independently. He had no one around to tell him to clean out the cabinets, so he didn't.

But it must hurt Josie to see her father living this way. "Your dad is who he is, Josie. You'll have to accept that."

"I can help him get set up better," she murmured. "I know he doesn't want me to pry too much, but I can grab a few things at the store to replace the bad stuff."

"If you give me the list, I'll shop for you," Gabe offered.

"Joe's asked me three times if I'm done banging around in here," she muttered. "He's got to be craving a cigarette."

"We could both go."

"Okay. Soon as I'm done here." Josie bent to her hands and knees and peered inside some lower cabinets, scrunching her nose when she pulled out a smashed box of spaghetti mix. She tossed that on the countertop, then reached back inside.

"Want help?"

She stood on her knees and let out a little groan. "God, no. I hate for you to watch me doing this."

"Why?"

"Because it's grimy and disgusting. Why don't you go talk to Joe. Tell him I'll be finished in five minutes."

Gabe started for the doorway, but paused when he noted Josie's smile for him. He wished he could return for a big, smacking thank-you kiss.

But he knew better.

And wished he didn't.

Joe's bedroom was in the opposite hallway from the kitchen. He lay propped on several pillows with his eyes closed and his hands clasped around his damned smokes. When Gabe entered, he opened his eyes.

"Hello again, Joe. Josie says you're sick."

"I'm fine. Cold air irritates my bronchial tubes."

Gabe glanced at the window beyond Joe's head. "You don't have storm windows?"

"Nope."

"They'd cut down the draft in here."

"Mebbee."

Gabe could get some good thermal panes at cost, but he already knew better than to ask the old man for permission. He'd have to just show up here with the windows, tell Joe they were leftovers and put them on. Josie could help install them.

Joe dropped the cigarette pack on his night table

and used his elbows to shove himself up, looking as though he was going to get out of bed.

"Stay there," Gabe said.

"Got comp'ny."

"We'll be gone soon."

Joe's gaze was stern. "I do better if I don't stay horizontal too long. That's why I sleep on that stack of pillows."

Gabe helped him up and stood back while the old man slid a heavy flannel shirt on over his cotton T-shirt. "I told the girl I needed to be up, but she wouldn't listen." Joe shot Gabe an incredulous look. "She's taken over my kitchen!"

Gabe's dad had been sick for several years. He knew there were times for taking extra care and times for maintaining respectful distances. Even if Joe was sicker than he realized, he wasn't ready to abandon his efforts to make his everyday motions. As well he shouldn't, until he was ready.

Josie wouldn't recognize that. She'd been a young college student when her mother had died, and she hadn't realized her mother was living out her last months. Her sister Isabel had tackled the burden of caring for their mother. Josie had dealt with guilt ever since.

That was probably why she was here, doing more than she should for a man who had done diddly-squat for her.

"What's she up to in there?" Joe asked. "She's been clattering around, slamming drawers."

"She's trying to help you."

"I didn't ask for anyone's help."

"I'll tell her to cool it, but I think you ought to let her do something."

Joe frowned for a moment, then nodded. "Maybe you're right. I can't get women. Even that girl out there, who claims to be uncomplicated."

Gabe laughed. "She's anything but that."

As the old guy buttoned his shirt, he indicated with a nod that Gabe should close the bedroom door. Then he spoke softly. "You and Josie-girl in trouble?"

"She'd say no. I say yes."

"Why?"

Gabe listened at the door for a moment, and when he heard the squeak of a cabinet door, he sat at the end of Joe's bed. "I'm in love with your daughter," he said. "I guess you can tell?"

"Ayuh."

"Well, we've been friends for a long time, and she's afraid that if we get involved we'll mess things up."

Joe finished dressing and sat at the head of the bed. "Do you think you would?"

"I never thought I'd say this, but I believe that Josie and I would make the fun and romance last." He grinned wryly at Joe.

"But she doesn't agree."

Gabe gave a slight nod.

"That girl has a mind of her own, like Ella Blume. Did you know her mama?"

"No. I met Josie when her mother was sick, but Ella died before I got a chance to meet her. Josie always said she didn't want to subject me to her mother."

"I don't blame her," Joe said. "Ella was...interesting. I'll just say that."

"What happened between you and Josie's mom?" Gabe asked.

"I watched Ella," Joe said. "Everyone talked about her, so I was surprised to discover that she was pretty. Had a nice figure. Had me curious." He hesitated, chuckling, then went on. "Sometimes I thought I noticed her looking at me. But then she'd just tell me I was doing something wrong. I decided I was imagining things."

"Complicated."

"Oh, yeah."

"And that one afternoon, she approached you?"

Joe widened his eyes in the same way his daughter did sometimes. "She just drove up, got out and knocked at the door. Came in like she visited me every day, then kissed me. Afterward, she didn't say boo. Not when she dressed. Not ever."

"She was confused."

"She was lonely, even if she was married," Joe argued. "And she was aware of what she was doing. She acted with purpose. I realize now that I was only a pawn in her game."

"You never got involved with another woman, Joe?"

"Nope."

Gabe couldn't imagine living to Joe's age and having had only one intimate experience. One unsatisfactory experience. How did a person greet each day with hope when they'd led such a lonesome life?

"What's going on in there?" Josie pushed the door

open. When she saw that Gabe and her father were simply talking, she studied Joe. "You're up?"

"He says it helps him feel better," Gabe said.

"It does?"

"I'm not coughing now, am I?"

"Okay, get up, then. We're leaving, anyway." She glanced back at her father as she left his bedroom. "But we'll be back in a half hour."

Joe shuffled out behind them. When Josie grabbed the trash sack full of discarded food she'd left near the front door, he grabbed at its edge. "What you got there? Is that my food?"

"It's just some old, rotten food you had in your cabinets," Josie said. "You'd get sick if you ate it."

Joe sank in his chair and glowered at Gabe, as if to send the message that they were supposed to be buddies now.

"We'll replace it," Gabe promised.

"I don't have the money for a bunch of new food."

"We do," Josie said. "We'll cover it just this once. It'll be a Christmas present. And yours to me will be to eat better and take care of yourself."

He looked at Gabe again.

Gabe nodded. "Let her do this," he murmured.

"Suit yourself." Joe waved them toward the door.

Ten minutes later, Gabe pushed a cart around the nearest grocery store while Josie scanned the canned goods aisle. "He didn't have any vegetables at all. Can you believe that?"

"He might not care for them, Josie."

"He'll like them if I come over and cook them!"

Hopefully, she wouldn't hover too much and drive the old guy crazy. "Consider the choices he's made, kid. I realize you want to be a part of your father's life, but don't be too intrusive or you'll push him away."

She dropped six cans of green beans into the cart. "He has no idea that he needs someone to care for him. How would he, if he's never experienced it?"

Did Josie hear herself?

Gabe bit his tongue and let her load the cart however she wished. He also found himself watching her as she analyzed the nutrition labels on the canned corn.

He used to tell her everything. Now he could tell her nothing about what was happening in his life, because his feelings for her were all mixed up in his perspective of it. Most of the time, she acted unaware of any changes.

She also didn't know he was eyeing her butt.

Gabe felt himself grow hard as he followed that sexy derriere around the corner to aisle six. If she were his wife, he'd help her carry the bags inside wherever they were living, then attack her just beyond the door.

They'd have hot sex among the warming milk and rolling cans. The fantasy was divine frustration. Was his choice to be patient with her the right one?

Or did he follow Josie's plan, and force his affection despite the loved one's protests?

"You daydreaming?" Josie asked. She set a huge carton of oatmeal in the basket and nudged Gabe out of the way, shoving the cart toward the front. After paying, she and Gabe loaded the groceries in his car trunk, then she got into the passenger side.

Ignoring his new grocery fantasy, Gabe helped her take the bags in to Joe's. They filled the cabinets and stayed long enough to eat some deli chicken with her father.

Josie was quiet as they walked back out to their vehicles.

"You want to come over?" he asked as he stood at the door to her truck. "The Chiefs game is over, I'm sure, but we could find something else to do."

He'd said that dozens of times before. They found something to watch on television or just hung out.

Today, he saw images of a naked Josie in his big, warm bed. Or his bigger, warmer bathtub.

"I'm beat. I should head home," she said.

"I'll follow you."

She rolled her eyes. "I can make it home, Gabe."

He nodded, then thought of another reason to follow her. "Didn't Callie, Ethan and the kids come over last night to help you put up your tree?"

She sighed. "You're just dying to see it, huh."

"You said you really liked this one."

Twelve minutes later, he'd admired Josie's usual red ball ornaments and Luke's popcorn strings and the new angel tree topper. Josie was rushing him through his admiring comments.

He didn't want to leave, damn it. Not now, when Josie was obviously in need of…convincing. That was what he wanted, wasn't it? To finally convince her that she required more from him than only friendship.

But then again, he'd hate to push too hard, and encourage retreat.

"You okay?" he asked.

"I will be." She whirled from the tree to stare out the window at the dark night. "God, did you see his kitchen?" she asked. "He has a total of two plates and four forks to his name."

"He's gotten along all right so far," Gabe said. "He might not be the healthiest person, but he doesn't look as if he's starving."

A small pinch formed between her eyes. Then she nodded. "Thanks." She drifted forward for a hug.

Perhaps Josie managed to hold her feelings to the same warm, amiable ones from the past.

Gabe felt a kick of desire. He hugged and withdrew, reserving those fantasies for a better time.

"I'm fine," Josie repeated. "But I can't help wondering if I'll wind up like him. Alone in this house with my beers and excuses."

No. She wouldn't. Father and daughter were both stubbornly independent, but Josie cared about people. She wouldn't hole up and allow the world to disappear. She wouldn't deny her own family.

She also made better choices for herself, whether she recognized it or not.

Gabe would let her form her own opinions about her relationship with her father. There would be time for this discussion later, when Josie's emotions weren't apt to come spilling out.

She shivered, and he drew her into his embrace again, intending to hold her only until she was still.

But instead of settling her head against his shoulder, she lifted it, seeking his mouth with her own.

Sending a jolt of powerful and specific need from Gabe's lips to his soul.

He might have curbed the kiss, but Josie sure as hell didn't. She kissed with eager passion. With emotion.

For a moment.

Then she moved her head past his, cuddling her face against his chest. "Sorry. I broke my own rule," she murmured. "I guess I needed to grab on to some of your strength for a minute."

Gabe heard the excuse, but he was still back at the kiss.

Josie had kissed him the way a woman kisses a man she loves and desires—almost as if her body understood what her heart and head didn't.

The vulnerabilities that this search had exposed had made him realize he felt more than friendship for Josie. Ironically, Josie's all-consuming goal to know her dad had left her too weary and confused to judge her own feelings.

Gabe saw it now, though. Clearly. Josie loved him, too, in that way. He knew she did.

That was enough.

Chapter Twelve

Gabe's arms encircled Josie's back and legs, then he lifted her, carrying her across to her sofa and lowering her lengthwise across it. Before she'd had time to think at all, he knelt beside her and continued the kiss she'd started.

She couldn't fathom stopping him, and not only because she'd invited his actions with her boldness. She kept her eyes closed, loving the exquisite warmth of Gabe's body and mouth as he trapped her against the sofa cushions. He was so talented with those lips.

He inched them away from hers. "Josie?"

She opened her eyes. He was right there, studying her, those beautiful blues formed into a query.

In answer, she reached around and hooked a palm around his neck, tugging his face back down to hers.

Josie realized she'd have to stop, but she couldn't yet. Gabe's kisses were too mind-boggling, his attention too satisfying. When his tongue touched her lips and then retreated, she followed it with hers. She was even fine with tongues for now.

Then he opened his mouth wider, tasting her.

Devouring her worries with his searing sexuality.

She decided that tongues were more than fine. Tongues were brilliant.

When Gabe shifted his kisses to a tender spot below her right ear, she surprised herself with a burst of laughter. Who'd have known they would kiss so well together?

"What's so funny?" he growled as he eased his hands beneath the hem of her shirt.

His move was potent. He hadn't asked. He hadn't hesitated or warned her.

She felt an ache grow, deep in her middle.

Was he really doing this?

Was Gabe Thomas really rubbing his thumbs over her lace-clad nipples? *Plucking* at them?

She stopped smiling. She could barely remember to breathe. As she watched his hands maneuvering beneath the material of her sweatshirt, she wondered if she'd ever seen anything so erotic. Until she noted Gabe's face and realized he was watching his hands, too.

His eyes were brilliant, his expression full of want.

He hadn't asked for permission to proceed.

But he was taking control.

Josie's sex spasmed.

She tugged at her sweatshirt hem, raising it until her flesh was exposed to him. Willing him to shove the lace aside and touch naked skin.

To taste her.

And Gabe, good man, did exactly as she wished. He stuck his thumbs beneath the band of her bra and glided it upward. Then he swooped down, pulling her nipple into his mouth. He suckled her.

That ache grew to a hard tension.

She couldn't breathe.

He lifted to inspect the wet, excited tip, then stared brazenly into Josie's face. "I knew you'd be beautiful, there," he murmured, his voice husky and sweet.

Josie shook her head, overwhelmed by the intimacy. Closing her eyes, she willed away the unwanted refusals and allowed herself to simply feel as he nibbled and toyed with her body, pausing only once to whisper about how much he loved what was happening between them.

This was okay. Manageable.

Josie was neither prude nor virgin.

Gabe wasn't close enough. He'd remained in the spot where he'd landed, next to the sofa on his knees. He touched her with only his hands, mouth and chest.

She yearned to feel him—all of him—against all of her.

"Come up here," she whispered.

Gabe wiped wetness from her nipple with his thumb, his pleasure wonderfully apparent, then he leaned close to press a soft kiss against her mouth. "With you, on that tiny sofa?" he asked.

She bucked her hips slightly. "With me, on this tiny sofa," she whispered.

Gabe kissed her again, but also settled on top of her, adjusting his long legs around hers.

When she felt his arousal pressing into her lower belly, her body reacted. Her wanting was stronger. Almost violent.

Sweet mercy.

He kissed her neck, her ear, her jaw while he eased his erection between her legs. He was right there. Ready for her. Hot. Hard.

Willing.

It would be so simple. If she stayed quiet. Let things go on. Relaxed in his heat. In his need for her.

She'd have what she ached for.

Sex.

With Gabe.

Sex with a man who knew her very soul.

With a man who loved her.

Whom she loved already.

What was she doing?

Josie shoved at his chest.

"What? Am I too heavy?"

Too heavy. Too real. Too…dear.

"Yes!"

When Gabe rolled off the couch and back to his knees, she jockeyed over him and strode into her kitchen, as if some Sheetrock and wooden beams could keep her from diving back into his arms and grabbing at what she wanted.

After finding a glass from her cabinet, she filled it with water and drank slowly, attempting to slake one thirst by satisfying another.

"You're not ready," Gabe said.

She didn't turn around. Whenever Gabe talked to her in her kitchen, he leaned against a certain spot at the counter, next to her fridge.

She knew where he was.

She couldn't fathom what he meant. Ready for

what? Did he think sex was inevitable between them? Or was he talking about something more?

She was afraid to ask.

Gabe belonged in that spot next to her fridge.

The thoughts and questions about sex were out of place.

She set the glass next to the sink and turned around. Gabe stood with his arms folded in front of him, looking rumpled. To-die-for sexy.

He wore an expression of determination.

She might as well talk about what had happened. Gabe would never leave until they had analyzed the question out of it. The man loved dang discussions lately.

But Josie would lead this conversation, and decide when it was finished. "Sorry. My fault," she said.

"What was? The starting or the stopping?"

"Both. Probably."

He held her gaze for a moment, one eyebrow lifted. "Okay. Maybe you had something to do with the starting," she said.

"You bet I did."

Josie tried not to notice, but Gabe was still aroused. He looked as if he was prepared to make love to her whenever she said the word—a minute ago, in two days.

Right now against the kitchen counter.

Hadn't she dreamed something like that once?

She pretended ignorance. "At least you got my mind off Joe's dismal eating habits."

"At least."

She crossed to the fridge beside him, just as she'd

done a hundred times before. However, a new awareness of Gabe made her movements jerky.

"We're okay," he said. He reached around her to grab a cola, an action *he'd* done a hundred times before. The informality comforted her. "You still going to that group lunch thing on Wednesday?" he asked.

A normal question. Thank God.

Some of the crew on the Kramer project had planned to eat out together in Wichita's Old Town, to celebrate the end of their huge collective effort. The construction crews had finished a week ago. Josie would finish decorating the last model by the beginning of the new year.

"I am."

"Good. I'll see you then if not before."

Josie wondered if she imagined a deeper warmth in his expression.

She would always wonder.

She could never ask.

"Thanks for the drink," he said, lifting it.

"Thanks for helping with Joe."

Gabe held her gaze just a hint longer than necessary, then nodded. "I'd better head home. I have an early meeting with the bread folks about that new office wing."

Josie didn't walk him out. She seldom did, and it felt natural to be casual. But after he'd left the kitchen, she waited until she'd heard his car start up and leave.

Then she wandered into the living room and sat on the sofa, peering down at the cushion and resting her palm against it.

As if she could still feel Gabe's heat.

She could have made love to him, tonight.

Josie scanned her dark living room, until the unlit tree caught her attention. Noticing a tilt on the new tree topper, she crossed the room to correct it.

An angel. Her mother had always insisted on a star, but Josie liked the angel.

Gabe deserved an angel as beautiful as he was, inside and out. Not a wisecracking, beer-drinking tomboy. Not a woman who might be on her way to alcoholism, despite her mother's warnings.

A woman who might very well wind up in a small house, with one chair and a television.

If Josie let herself love Gabe and he grew weary of her quirks, how would he tell her?

When she'd adjusted the angel, Josie nodded at it. "You know I'm right, don't you?" she asked, frowning at the doll's porcelain smile.

After plugging in the cord to light the hundreds of white bulbs, Josie stood back to admire her tree. She opened her drapes then, sending a picture of holiday merriment out into the darkness.

Few people would be around to enjoy the decorations on her tree. The neighborhood was still sparsely populated, even after all these years. Josie didn't care. She'd lit the tree and opened the curtains because it made her happy to do so, and she wouldn't abandon her favorite pleasures in life because of her choices.

Yes, she'd done the right thing about Gabe. She knew that, if nobody else would.

Soon, this pinch of physical emptiness would lessen, as well as her loneliness.

She was certain.

"CAN I OPEN the green one next?" Luke asked, turning quickly to get his mother's approval before he unwrapped another of his gifts.

At Callie's go-ahead, Luke tore off the paper, crumbled it into a loose ball and tossed it backward as he gasped over a new toy helicopter. The paper landed in the knee-high flood of Christmas wrap, bows and toys that had deluged Ethan and Callie's family room.

The white, velvety bow fell near Lilly as she sat playing with a new toy phone. As she picked up the bow to examine it, her ability to focus was apparent. The bow's wide, twisted pattern would probably keep her enthralled for several minutes.

She sat up on her own now. She cackled, sometimes, at Luke's big-brother antics. She hadn't spoken yet, but Callie said that her little girl had a lot of catching up to do.

Ethan believed she'd be a star kindergartner in a few years. He suspected that she would excel at science, like her mother. Already, she paid attention to details.

The seizures had vanished with the B6 treatments. Everything else would follow.

When Josie had sat down cross-legged on the floor near both children, she'd intended to help them open their gifts, but they hadn't needed her. Luke's fingers were growing nimble, and Lilly preferred to concentrate on her things one at a time.

Despite the children's independence, the morning had been a crazy one in the Taylor home. Ethan and

Callie had invited Josie to sleep in their guest room last night so she could enjoy the kids' Santa surprise.

Of course, that meant they'd all been awakened before dawn, when Ethan's quarrel with Luke had escalated past whispers. Ethan had kept saying that five-fifteen was too early, even on Christmas. Luke had kept saying that Santa had already been here—he'd peeked—so it was fine.

When Josie had then heard Lilly's cries from her crib and Callie's murmured responses, she'd come out of her room to encourage the adults to start the party.

It was six now and the kids had nearly finished with their gifts. Ethan had disappeared into the kitchen seconds ago, presumably to prepare his speciality—French toast.

Although Josie was expected to stay the entire day, she was ready to go home. She wasn't hungry, she wanted more sleep and she craved alone time. Maybe she was getting sick.

After the earliest breakfast she could remember eating in a while, Josie watched Ethan and Callie sit together on their sofa to open gifts. She was happy for them. Yet they made her feel lonely.

Rick and Brenda's arrival in the early afternoon didn't help. Their presence put Josie in the oddball seat again. Then, immediately after dinner, Isabel telephoned, speaking excitedly about her morning with twenty-three members of Trevor's family.

After she'd handed the phone to Callie, Josie made up a plate of food for Joe and used it as an excuse to leave. She knew her father would be home. He'd told her that he didn't care for all the hoopla.

He was as full of poppycock as she was sometimes.

Joe was at home, but he'd obviously found his favorite way to celebrate. The endless string of smokes and drinks had left him too bleary-eyed and queasy to eat the plate of food. Josie placed it in his fridge and helped him into bed, after hiding the cigarettes in a kitchen cupboard.

Disappointed, Josie returned to her quiet house and took a long nap.

The next week, she worked hard on the Kramer project, managing to meet her final deadline and refusing to scan the street in front of the houses, looking for Gabe's car. He'd finished his part of the job and moved on.

On New Year's Day morning, her phone awakened her. She managed to ignore the ring, knowing the machine would pick up, but then her cell phone started ringing. That would have to be Callie.

Josie had left the phone in her bag, so she trotted through the house to the front door, where she'd dropped her purse on Saturday evening after work. She grabbed the phone and clicked it on. "Everything okay, Cal?"

"Sure it is," Callie said. "Ethan's feeding the kids, so I had a minute. I thought I'd missed you. You awake?"

Josie glanced at the clock and mewed something noncommittal. It was after ten, so she certainly should have been up and around.

Callie chuckled. "If you're still in bed, you must have had a good time at your party last night. Ethan and I expected you to drop by ours. He invited a new work buddy who was hoping to meet you."

Her sister had assumed that Josie had gone out to celebrate with Gabe last night, as she usually did. Callie must also think that Ethan had neglected to tell her about his work buddy. But Ethan had told her. She just hadn't cared.

"Oh. Well." Josie stopped herself, having no clue what to say.

"Never mind," Callie said, laughing again. "I know your social calendar is full and I'm truly not offended. I just wanted to wish you a happy New Year."

Josie returned the wish and hung up feeling as if she'd lied to her sister. She'd thought she might go to Callie and Ethan's annual gathering. She'd bought some chips and beer to take along, and she'd even decided to wear her sophisticated black sweater.

She'd thought she should be ready to meet an available man and start dating again. She'd told herself that surely some really great kisses could make her forget Gabe's.

But she hadn't been able to convert all those mights and shoulds to a true desire to go. She'd sat in her nice sweater at home, eating the chips, drinking the beer and wallowing.

She'd fallen asleep on the sofa at eleven o'clock.

Now she maneuvered around her Christmas tree to open her curtains before heading for the shower.

A knock sounded at the door.

She might be tempted to ignore it, but the person outside must have seen her open the curtains. Josie glanced down at her tank top and panties.

It had to be Gabe out there.

Heat flooded her limbs. Wouldn't it be fun to open the door as she was, then run to her bed to see if he followed?

Sighing, Josie stepped closer to the door to check the peephole.

Sure enough.

"Hang on a sec," she hollered. "I'm not decent."

There was a silence, so Josie peeked again. Gabe peered at the door, his expression serious and also sort of…pained.

Chortling, Josie trotted to her bedroom to jump into a pair of jeans. A year ago, she might have met Gabe at the door like this—in jeans and tank top.

No matter how much she kept telling herself that things between her and Gabe hadn't changed, they had. She could only deal with it.

After pulling a flannel shirt from her closet, she slipped it on and buttoned it on her way out. When she opened her front door, Gabe's eyes barely touched her face before they dropped to her chest. "You're dressed."

"I know." They stared at each other. Then Josie noticed the dusting of snow on the ground behind him and realized it was very cold. She shoved the door open wider. "Get in here, Gabe."

He entered, closed the heavy door behind him and stopped, two feet inside.

"You here for a reason?" she asked.

"I expected you last night at Mom's party."

"I told you I had other plans."

"And the lady insists that she isn't avoiding me."

She turned toward her tree, ignoring the comment as she pretended she simply had to adjust Luke's popcorn strands a week after the holiday's passing.

Yes, she had been avoiding Gabe. And it hadn't worked. She still thought about him all the time.

She could still feel his hands on her body.

His kisses everywhere.

Almost everywhere.

Honestly? She longed to feel them everywhere.

"How was Callie and Ethan's shindig?" Gabe asked.

She was tempted to say something noncommittal and let his assumption pass, but as she plucked a Mickey Mouse ornament from its spot and moved it two inches, she decided she was too tired to fib. "I didn't go," she muttered.

He heard her. "What'd you do?"

"I stayed here, okay?" She faced Gabe. Tall, sexy Gabe, with his black leather coat and too-blue eyes. "I listened to CDs and had a great time right here at home. You always said I should learn to spend time alone."

His expression didn't change into one of great surprise. He shifted his weight. "Mom and my sisters asked about you."

"How was their party?"

"Fine, until about eleven, when I left. I was in bed by midnight."

"Alone?" she asked, though she shouldn't have. It'd slipped out.

"Alone." He grinned now, and she couldn't help but respond.

"What're you doing today?" she asked.

"I usually sleep late and watch the games, but you know that. Do you have plans?"

"No, but I have an idea."

"Uh-oh."

She chuckled, enjoying the teasing. "I'd like to spend time with Joe today, but not at his house, where he can miss all his bad habits. I want to bring him here."

Gabe nodded, and she felt as if her old buddy was back, listening to her plan and supporting her efforts.

"I could pull together a dinner. I bought some ham slices and canned black-eyed peas that I could fancy up."

"Sounds good. Joe's lucky to have you in his corner."

"Would you mind picking him up? I'll call to warn him, and you could be back here at, say, two."

"I'm invited?"

Of course he was. Now that he was here, teasing her and supporting another spur-of-the-moment plan, she couldn't imagine this day without him. "That's what I meant."

"I just thought—"

"Don't, Gabe," Josie interrupted. "Just…be…*normal*. Okay?"

He gave a slow nod. "I could bring some cranberry muffins my mother sent home with me, and I have some beer."

"No. No alcohol."

Gabe faked a shocked expression and Josie laughed. "I can't believe I just said that, either, but Joe doesn't limit amounts when he drinks. I worry about him."

"Cranberry and beer aren't a good mix, anyway," Gabe said. "…Muffins and sodas it is."

Gabe left, and Josie went back to her bedroom to strip, shower and re-dress.

Joe couldn't be more than what he was, but Josie saw something her mother must not have had time to recognize: a sweet soul who had welcomed his unknown daughter immediately and who'd hung a wreath on his door despite the many years he must have spent the holiday alone.

Did all these feelings add up to a sense of loving him?

She wasn't certain.

But she yearned to love him. That was enough.

She shouldn't love Gabe, either. Not in this new way. Being near him was risky now, and would require more willpower than she'd ever had cause to exercise.

She'd have to get better at resisting impulses.

However, inviting him to dinner was a considered choice, and surely more natural than the past few weeks of avoiding him. Perhaps today could be a new start for all of them: for herself with Gabe. For Joe.

Chapter Thirteen

"He's asleep?"

At Josie's whisper, Gabe yanked his attention from the bowl game on television and glanced beside him, realizing that Joe had drifted off.

"I don't think he's a huge football fan," Gabe muttered, then frowned when he saw the uncomfortable droop to the old man's head. "His neck's going to get sore."

"We'd better move him." Josie guided her dad's head on down to the armrest while Gabe lifted his legs onto the cushions. After Josie had located a crocheted afghan in a wicker container and placed it over her father, she and Gabe stood watching Joe, who was snoring softly.

"Want me to take off his shoes?" Gabe asked.

"No," Josie murmured. Then, with a jerk of her head, she summoned Gabe to follow her.

He started worrying when he realized she was leading him back to her bedroom. Once inside, she closed the door behind him and smiled at his expression. "Chill, Gabe. Weren't you following that game?"

"Sure. The Wildcats were up by sixteen."

"Okay, then." She turned to click on the small television on her dresser, then kicked off her shoes and flopped belly-up on her double bed.

Gabe remained near the doorway.

"Oh, relax," she said. "I was into the game, too. And we've done this before. Remember the time when Luke was really little and fell asleep on my living-room floor? We snuck in here and watched TV for hours. It was some Carol Burnett marathon, if I recall correctly."

Right. And it had been Lucille Ball, not Carol Burnett. But Gabe hadn't been on this bed with Josie since he'd fallen for her.

They were pretending that hadn't happened, though. Because Josie needed a friend rather than a lover.

Gabe lay down beside her, rested his hands behind his head and directed his eyes toward the television set.

He certainly couldn't lose himself in the game and forget who was next to him. The football wives of the world should rejoice.

When the Wildcats' running back ran thirty-two yards and Josie didn't react, Gabe realized she wasn't paying much attention to the game, either. Usually, she'd be up on her feet, jumping around, hooting and hollering.

Maybe he'd conduct a teeny little test.

Slowly, he inched his calf closer to hers and touched her leg. Then he wriggled around some, as if repositioning himself to get comfortable. He managed to connect the two of them from thigh to foot.

She didn't jerk away, but she did sit up to grab the remote from the bedside stand and turn up the volume.

Maybe she *was* watching the game.

When she lay back down, he caught a whiff of her scented bath soap. She smelled clean.

She'd be warm and soft. Scrumptious.

Gabe thought about lace. And voluptuous boobs. He'd never known how erotic it was to catch a glimpse of pale-pink lace beneath the clothes of a self-professed tomboy. How it made a man hanker to peel off the outer layers to find the wicked and delightful creature beneath.

He was getting an erection. He'd have a tough time ridding himself of it with Josie here beside him.

He certainly couldn't hide it.

He couldn't even check to see if it was obvious.

This just-friends-even-though-we-are-both-attracted plan was impossible. Didn't she understand that?

"Josie."

"Gabe…"

They'd spoken at the same time. Josie lifted onto her elbows and made the peaks beneath her shirt even more enticing.

Gabe forgot what he'd been about to say.

"You go first," she said.

He snorted, then searched for a phrase. What would convince her that she'd be okay, that *they* would be okay? That little could be worse than this repetitive stopping and starting?

"I think we ought to—"

"Shhh," she soothed, staring at his mouth. "No

promises. That's a rule I have to hang on to, okay? No promises. If we do this, it's only because we haven't been able to avoid it."

Do this. She made that sound so hot.

"You think not?" he asked.

"I know not."

Groaning, he rolled over on top of her, meeting her mouth at the same time his full body met the length of hers. And he kissed the doubt out of her, or tried to, letting her feel everything he hadn't said.

That he wanted her too much to resist her.

That her wanting him was okay. It was great, in fact.

That they were surely made for each other.

Couldn't she sense that? They were a perfect fit.

He'd bet his new car they were a perfect fit in every way. But he wasn't sure if she was agreeing to anything beyond kisses. Maybe a touch. A glimpse of lace.

The kisses were fine, though.

Theirs lingered and changed and heated with every second.

Before Gabe went any further with his mouth or hands, he backed up to gauge Josie's reaction again. This wouldn't be a good time to get slugged.

Her eyes were huge, her lips parted. She didn't utter a single refusal. In fact, she reached out to grab his shirt and yank him back down to her.

Gabe spent long moments just lying on top of Josie, kissing her. She was willing, even though his arousal throbbed, thick and needy between them.

Had she moved the line?

How far?

Gabe felt her hands crawl beneath his shirt in back, then she smoothed them along his muscles as they kissed.

Apparently, hands against skin were okay.

Gabe slid his beneath her shirt to find that lace. Her breasts felt so full, her nipples so reactive. They'd hardened at his slightest touch.

He nudged the cloth of her shirt aside. "Mmmm. Red today."

She raised her head a fraction. "What?"

"Red lace. Last time you wore pink."

"Gabe!" That name shout was surely a reprimand, but her bright face sent a different message.

Did a woman wear a sexy bra if she didn't hope someone would notice it? Gabe tugged the lace down slightly to expose her perfect rose-brown nipples, relishing the way the fabric pushed at her hard nubs.

Finally, he bent down, kissing and tasting her until she was squirming beneath him.

They'd been here before.

Gabe rocked his hips, nudging against Josie's heat and she moaned, rocking with him. Accepting the new closeness. Adjusting her legs for hotter access.

The line had moved quite a bit.

Gabe closed his eyes and concentrated. He wouldn't allow anything to happen on this bed until Josie communicated that she was okay with it. He could go slow.

She put her hand on Gabe's chest and coasted it slowly downward, until she was caressing his arousal through his pants.

This was slow?

Opening his eyes, he caught her "gotcha" smile.

He nearly came unhinged when she fingered the fastener to his pants. His heart pounding fast, he kissed her, his tongue surging deep against her panting breaths.

Mimicking the act of sex.

Aching for it.

This fire between them burned so hot. Did she not realize this was rare? That some people couldn't combine a true liking with total passion?

He swooped down to nibble on her neck, at the same time undoing her jeans. Then he slid his fingers beneath more lace to touch her curls for the first time.

"You're so beautiful."

"Hey! Z'anyone there!"

"Oh, no. He's awake." Josie scrambled off the bed to yank her bra up over her breasts, pull down her shirt and fasten her pants.

By the time Gabe had simply gathered his wits, she was starting for the door.

And by the time he'd walked into Josie's living room, she was helping her father into his coat. "He wants to go home," she murmured, glancing at Gabe. "He's insisting."

"I'll take you, Joe. Hang on a sec." Gabe strode into the kitchen and grabbed a Tupperware container from the fridge. Josie had made her father a plate of leftovers.

When Gabe returned to the living room, Josie gave him that soft-eyed look he recognized as a thanks. He handed the plate to Joe, donned his coat and pressed a kiss against Josie's forehead on his way out.

He didn't say he'd be back. He wasn't sure he'd be

welcome. Would Josie ignore what had happened this afternoon? Or, worse, retreat again? All he could think about as he drove the quiet old man home was that he had to get back to Josie's before she'd had time to move her damn line again.

"You two going to get married?" Joe asked, breaking into Gabe's visions of red lace and brown nipples.

He glanced at Joe, wondering if the old man had heard them in the bedroom.

But Joe faced forward, sleepy-eyed and serious. He appeared to be making conversation.

"Josie and I? We're still just friends, really."

"That's what Josie-girl says, too."

Josie would call these interludes beyond friend status as slip-ups, probably. Gabe would call them brief forays into greater living.

The old man stared out the windshield. "Mother knew I'd been with Ella in that way. She said I was a fool."

"Did she ask about the pregnancy?"

"No. No one ever said anything to me. I believe Mom had suspicions, though."

Gabe nodded, remembering his own mother's speculations.

They'd all behaved badly, hadn't they?

"I want to be good to Josie." The old guy paused, then added, "It's hard to change at my age."

Perhaps. Sometimes the war could be won with a succession of smaller battles. As far as Gabe could tell, Joe hadn't tried very hard to curb his habits.

Gabe managed to walk Joe to his door and wish him

a nice evening, but then he jumped in his car and raced to Josie's house with a speed that might turn even her knuckles white. To hell with his vow to be a friend. He wanted more, and he was willing to make a valiant effort to convince her that he was right.

She opened the door in the nude.

Laughing at his expression, she ran down the hallway and barely beat him to the bed. He didn't have any lace to peel, any lines to test, any resistance to collapse.

In moments, Gabe lay atop Josie, his hands framing her face and his erection braced at her sex. When he might have asked if she was ready, she brought her face to his, lifted her body.

Pulled him inside, even while he pushed.

And when he was fully inside her, Gabe had to stop for a moment. Josie felt so right. So good. His feeling for her was stronger than it had ever been.

Josie looked as intense as he felt. Her eyes were dark, her face sober.

Gorgeous.

Soon, she was helping him love her. Moving and kissing and making him laugh and growl and lose his breath.

Gabe couldn't count the times he made love to Josie that afternoon and evening. The experience was a marathon mixture of sensual surprises that left him satiated.

Yet wanting more.

If he tried, however, he might be able to count the words between them. When he'd whispered his affections to her, she'd informed him that it was boring to talk about love during sex.

That was okay. Knowing Josie, when the conversation did happen it would start and stop in bursts. In the meantime, Gabe could be happy just learning all the ways he could get her hot.

He'd keep her hot, too.

He'd been dating a lot longer than Josie, and he understood how to keep the zing in a good romance.

She'd kill him if she was aware that he was thinking that way. She'd always claimed that romance and love were myths maintained by woman's desire to nurture and man's longing to recreate himself.

Since they didn't plan to have children, she'd say, they didn't need to fall for those old tales. She must be telling herself that this was just a fling of another color.

But Josie was about to be wooed by a master.

"You want to do something tonight?" Gabe called from his bathroom, where the sound of his electric shaver had ceased just seconds earlier.

Wet-headed and shower-fresh, Josie stood near his closet and perused a small selection of her work clothes that had somehow migrated there. Her own closet was similarly integrated.

Already. After seventeen days.

Worse than that, one of their mutual work colleagues had asked her yesterday if she and Gabe had plans for Valentine's Day. They were recognized as a couple. She couldn't imagine how that had happened so fast.

The thought perturbed her enough that she jammed her hands on her hips and said, "No. I don't want to do something tonight."

Gabe poked his head around the door frame. "Why not?"

She buttoned into a crisp white blouse. "We can't keep being together every minute we aren't at work. We have lives. Active lives. I'm not the kind of person who neglects her friends and family for a man."

"Oh." He returned to the bathroom while she slipped into a navy suit. Soon, she heard the sound of him brushing his teeth. He'd brush for a minute, spit, gargle and then brush again.

Good heavens. She'd committed his personal habits to memory. When he appeared at her side to pull a black-striped shirt from a hanger, she turned to stare at him. "This will cool down. Flings do."

She repeated the gist of that statement nearly every time they were together, just to see how Gabe reacted. And maybe because a part of her wished he'd convince her that the opposite was true.

She couldn't believe she was thinking that way.

Gabe left his shirt hanging open and grabbed a pair of jeans from the back of a chair. He pulled them on, and as he zipped and buttoned the fly he gave her a wry look. "You and I can't be a fling by definition, Josie. We've been friends for too long."

"Then this is a…"

How could she think with that tanned, muscular chest right in front of her? Why did Gabe have to be so hunky?

She flung her hands up. "This is us getting the attraction out of our systems."

"Whatever you say."

Gabe went into his bathroom again and closed the door between them. Leaving her staring after him, craving more of an argument.

Followed by makeup kisses, and then sex.

There was something erotic about loving a man who knew her ins and outs.

Josie had spent every night with Gabe over the past seventeen days. Sometimes, he showed up at her door with a great bottle of wine. Other times, she picked up dinner and drove out to his house. After work last Friday they'd visited Joe and left late, only to steam up Gabe's car windows on a dirt road outside town.

They made love often, making creative use of their walls, beds and floors. Gabe had a thing about his clawfoot tub. She'd never taken so many baths in her life. Once, he'd done wicked things to her after lifting her onto his workroom bench.

For the rest of her life, she'd grin when she thought of that bench.

She probably had a thing now about that bench.

She'd never expected to fall this deeply in love. She'd considered herself incapable. She had a dang short attention span and she kept wondering when Gabe would tire of her and seek out a tall blonde.

The idea broke her heart.

Just to prove she could, she dropped by Callie and Ethan's house that evening and stayed to have dinner with the family. On Thursday morning, a vase of white roses was waiting on her porch when she stepped out to get her newspaper. She read the card, snickering at Gabe's ornery ditty. Then she kept the roses wrapped to take to her new job site. The bouquet would look beautiful in the accounting firm's reception area.

Gabe knew she hated getting flowers.

When she saw him that night, she reminded him of that fact, then punished him by insisting they finish the dinner dishes before she'd go to bed with him.

Afterward, she made him go home.

The next afternoon, he sent white lilies to her job site. This note was more specific about which of her body parts he'd missed. It made her laugh out loud, but she'd never tell him that.

What did all the white mean? She wasn't virginal. She'd think he'd send her red or purple. Some vibrant color.

She hired a courier to take the lilies to Callie. They were Cal's favorite, and made a nice thank-you for the other night's dinner.

That evening, she rang Gabe's doorbell. When he didn't answer right away, she let herself in with the key. They'd traded again. Probably a mistake.

When he appeared through the kitchen doorway, she said, "Stop sending the flowers, Gabe. You are very aware that I don't like it."

"Why not?"

"You know why not. I prefer relationships where I'm on equal terms with the man. I pay for myself. I make my own choices."

"So send *me* flowers."

She sighed. "Every guy says that to me. Do you know that?" she asked. "What are you doing, anyway? And why white?"

He lifted his shoulders. "If you stop giving them away, I'll tell you why I'm sending white flowers."

"Never mind." Josie turned to go.

He caught her arm. "You won't listen to what I tell you about us—about the way I feel, so maybe I have to show you."

"Don't."

She wound up staying with Gabe that night, but the next day she left before breakfast, telling Gabe she wanted to visit Joe. She hadn't seen her father in a while. She'd wondered about him.

Joe didn't answer her knock. She kept trying, then hollered for a while and finally returned to her truck to grab her cell phone. She sat inside the warm cab to telephone Gabe.

He picked up immediately, thank God.

"Joe's not coming to the door, but I know he's home," Josie said. "I'm worried that he's hurt in there."

"He hasn't given you a key?"

"I haven't asked for one."

"Get one when you can," he said. "And try knocking again. I'll be right there."

Gabe's car had appeared at the end of the street in minutes, but Josie was so intent on getting inside to her father that she barely acknowledged him.

"Joe!" she hollered, pressing her cheek against the thin door. No answer. She fisted her hand to knock again, but Gabe grabbed it.

He swore as he examined the angry chafing on her knuckles. "Is this from today?"

She glanced down. She hadn't realized it before, but her skin had broken open in a couple of spots. "Guess so."

"No gloves?"

Her knuckles stung now. She rubbed them with the opposite hand. "I thought I'd be running from the truck to his house."

Gabe stepped off the porch and crossed the yard to scrutinize a side window that led to the bathroom. "When we installed these storm windows, I noticed a busted latch on an inner frame. I'm going to break in."

"Whatever it takes."

Gabe ran to his car to grab a tool kit. After returning, he pulled out a screwdriver and pried off the storm-window frame. Within minutes, he'd made an opening large enough to crawl through. Then he boosted Josie up and in.

Fearing what she'd find, Josie dashed around to the front door to let Gabe in before she looked too hard for her father. Then Gabe took her hand and walked with her toward Joe's bedroom.

Her father was in bed. He wasn't asleep, yet he appeared very groggy. Josie approached his side. "You okay?"

His eyes were swollen to pink slits. "Fine, fine," he said. "Gonna sit up." His voice was pitched too high, his words slurred. He wouldn't hold Josie's gaze.

He was very drunk.

Josie traded a look with Gabe, noting his down-turned mouth. The sadness in his gaze.

She wasn't sure whether she was more angry or relieved.

Both of them watched Joe try to sit up.

"Lie still," Gabe said. He took an empty bottle from the night stand and showed it to Josie. "Did you drink all this, Joe?"

"Mebbee."

"When's the last time you ate something?" Josie asked.

"Doan' know."

"You can't live on Wild Turkey, Dad."

"Been doing 'zactly that for alotta years, Josie-girl." He lifted up again and bobbed his head around.

"Maybe you should get up," Josie said. "Gabe can help you to your chair while I fix you some coffee or something."

"Doan' care for coffee." As if to punctuate his statement, Joe started a bout of painful-sounding coughs that left him flat on his back again.

Gabe stalked out of the room and returned with a big bowl, in case Joe was sick to his stomach, but the coughs eventually subsided.

Josie left her father in his warm bed, but propped him up with pillows. She and Gabe made some hot chicken broth for Joe to sip, then spent the day tending to her sick father.

After that, she visited Joe every day. She kept thinking he could have died in his ramshackle little house, alone, while she spent her nonwork hours having sex with Gabe.

Gabe must have sensed her turmoil. They reverted

to more of a friendship without a discussion of the change. Gabe also visited her father when he could, and acted accepting of the fact that Josie's time and emotions were occupied.

He loved her only when she let him know she needed him, which was more often than she liked to admit.

Soon, she'd have to deal with the Gabe issue, too. Joe's illness made her feel she had no business pretending she could handle anything long-term.

Gabe had recognized that from the start. He shouldn't be surprised that her every effort was geared toward helping the old man she'd begun to think of as her dad.

Chapter Fourteen

His arms loaded with firewood, Gabe strode across his deck and entered the house. He dropped the logs on the hearth before returning to close the back door. As he took off his coat and draped it over the sofa back, he shivered, reacting belatedly to the frigid outside air. The high today had been two degrees, and that had been hours ago. It must be well below zero by now.

Just being outside made a person grit his teeth to withstand the fierceness of the temperature.

When Gabe had talked to Josie at lunchtime, she'd been as worried as usual about her father. She'd intended to drop by the old guy's place after work to check on him, then come here for a chili supper.

At least she'd recovered from her father's recent blackout. At first, Gabe had thought Josie would drive the old man further into the bottle. She'd kept going by to make endless pots of soup. She'd also snuck frequent peeks into the old guy's cabinets, hunting for the alcohol Joe couldn't afford, physically or financially.

So far, so good. Joe had settled into a healthier

routine. And Josie had relaxed, checking only every other day now and spending time with Gabe once more.

Thank heaven. He'd missed her. He understood her nervousness. He was better equipped to handle their romance, he supposed. His mother had married twice, loving both men wholeheartedly.

Josie might be a master avoider, but he hoped by Valentine's Day he'd manage to convince her that he wasn't planning on falling out of love with her.

After tossing a couple of crumpled newspaper sheets into the firebox, Gabe added kindling and a hefty stack of cedar logs. He wanted a roaring fire to last through the evening.

The phone rang before he'd had a chance to put a match to the newspaper.

"Gabe? It's Josie."

"Hi, babe," he said teasingly. She claimed to hate it when he called her that, but he thought she secretly liked it.

She was silent.

He frowned. "What's up?"

"It's my dad," she said, her voice small. "Something's wrong with him. I had to use my key to get in, and I found him…" She hesitated, and when she spoke again, she sounded as though she was crying. "He was curled in a ball. His lips were blue and he was talking gibberish again. I assumed he was drunk."

"He's not? Where is he?"

"He was on the kitchen floor, but they put him in the ambulance. They're transporting him to St. Joseph in Wichita."

Aw, hell. Poor Joe.

Poor Josie.

"At first, the technicians said it could be alcohol poisoning—I told them about the last time—but now they believe it's pneumonia. They say he could have died tonight."

"Are you going in the ambulance?"

"No. I'm, um…" She sighed. "They said it would be better if I found a ride. He might have to stay a while."

"I'll come get you. Hang on." Gabe shrugged into his heavy coat again and started immediately for her house.

Joe was stable by the time he and Josie had arrived at the hospital and located him. He'd been admitted to the emergency room, but the E.R. doc felt confident that they'd move him upstairs to a bed later this evening.

Indeed, he had a severe case of pneumonia, compounded greatly by the effects of his habits. The staff allowed Josie to say hello to her father, who complained more and more loudly as he grew more lucid. Afterward, they encouraged her to go home and return tomorrow. They said Joe would need rest tonight, more than company.

On the drive home, Josie slouched in the passenger seat, her expression pensive. "He could have died alone if I hadn't come by. He isn't in touch with his other family. I looked them up, but there are no other Henshaws in the book. I have no idea how to reach them."

Gabe did. He'd spoken to Alana briefly on New Year's Eve, when she'd dropped by his mother's party.

He hadn't told her that he was in touch with her son. Their estrangement was none of his business.

But Josie had a living grandmother she might enjoy, and that *was* Gabe's business. He'd never let on that he was aware of the connection. That he'd heard gossip about her family eons ago, and had suspected the truth all along.

He'd hoped that Joe would break the news, and Gabe wouldn't have to confess how much he knew about the family.

"At least you found him," Gabe told Josie now. "And maybe this will be an incentive for him to clean up. I get the impression he hates the lack of privacy in his hospital room. Surely he'll try to avoid any future emergency room visits."

"You think he'll be okay, then? He'll go home?"

"I believe so."

Josie didn't respond, and Gabe was approaching the outskirts of Augusta. The town looked locked up solid tonight. Everyone must be snuggled beneath blankets or cozying up to fires. Or both.

Where he'd planned to be with Josie. "Interested in warming up with some of my chili?" he asked as he neared the turn to her place.

"No. The hospital could call."

Gabe finished the journey to her house and parked in the drive. "You could warm me up without chili."

She gaped at him, showing a touch of the spirit he loved. "Oh, right, Gabe. Like I'd invite you in tonight."

He grinned. "I had to try. I'll pick you up in the morning. The hospital starts visiting hours at eight."

"Don't you work tomorrow?"

"I'll take the day off, same as you."

"Oh, Gabe…"

"No argument. Get inside. Stay toasty and expect me around seven-thirty."

She ran for her door.

After waiting until she'd gone inside and turned on a living-room light, Gabe continued on home to wrestle with his conscience. Alana might want to hear about her son's illness.

Josie deserved the whole truth about her family, even if it meant Gabe might be calling her wrath upon himself.

After finally lighting those cedar logs, Gabe made a phone call to his mother.

The next morning, he and Josie were at Joe's bedside by eight-thirty. They talked to him, but the old guy was in no mood for conversation. He pouted constantly, fussed with his tubes and grumbled a few earthy complaints about the gowns, the food and the constant interruptions.

When the attendants arrived with his breakfast, Gabe and Josie headed to the cafeteria downstairs for coffee and croissants.

And when they were waiting for the elevator to go back upstairs, they bumped into Alana.

"Hello there, Gabe and…Josie, isn't it? What brings you two here?"

Oh, Lord. Apparently, Gabe's mother had passed on the message that Joe was sick without telling Alana details about who had discovered him and called the ambulance.

"My dad is here," Josie said. "He has bacterial pneumonia—a severe case."

"Oh, I'm sorry," Alana said, her tone polite. "Will he be okay?"

"We think so," Josie said. "But when I found him on his kitchen floor yesterday, I wasn't so sure. We're going up to visit him now."

Alana stared at Gabe, her eyes wide and hazel. Why had Gabe not noticed their particular color and shape before?

If she'd never considered the idea that Josie was her granddaughter, she had now.

But Josie remained unaware.

"And why are you here today?" Josie asked. "Volunteer work?"

The elevator doors opened, and she allowed a couple of men to board in front of her while she waited for Alana's answer.

"Uh, well, no. My son's here," Alana croaked.

With a sense of impending doom, Gabe trailed behind Josie and her grandmother as they stepped onto the elevator. Everyone faced the doors, then eyed the lit buttons on the control panel. Seven wasn't lit. Alana, who was nearest to the panel, pushed the button and didn't bother to push one for him and Josie. She didn't sidle out of the way, either. She simply watched the doors close.

Josie chuckled. "Funny, we're going to the same floor."

Alana nodded.

People entered and exited on several floors, but by

the time the elevator had reached seven, the three of them were alone again. They filed out.

"Nice chatting with you, Mrs. Morgan," Josie said, starting down the hall. It took her six steps to realize that Alana was walking alongside her. Still, she simply tittered and kept going.

When Alana followed her into the room, Josie stopped to peer at her. "This is your son's room?" she asked.

"Well, hello, Mother," Joe said in a strong voice that sounded very much like Alana's.

The next hour was a scramble in Gabe's mind. Josie acted all right. She even talked to Alana some, maintaining that cordiality, and managed to make Joe laugh by promising to smuggle in a big, fat hamburger for his lunch tomorrow.

But as soon as they left the hospital room so her father could sleep, Josie grabbed Gabe's arm. "Did you have any idea that Alana Morgan had a son named Joe?"

Gabe was tired of trying to keep the story straight. He wanted Josie to know everything. But this wasn't a conversation for a hospital corridor.

He took Josie's arm and coaxed her into a vacant foyer. After motioning for her to sit in a padded rocking chair, he scooted another around in front of it. He didn't want a lot of space between them. If she could see his sincerity, his concern for her well-being, his love, then maybe she'd respond well to the truth.

"Yes, I did know, Josie. Alana has two sons and a daughter. I didn't remember at first, but after we met Joe I recognized the connection."

Josie scowled. "How could this happen? I thought he had no family—or none that cared. But it turns out they're your friends. And you *knew!*"

Gabe gripped the hands Josie held clenched on her thighs. "The Henshaws aren't my friends, really. They are acquaintances. And none of the family stayed in contact with your dad, so I did forget the connection."

Josie yanked her hands away and clasped them around her belly. "You're not helping."

He clenched his own hands, eyeing her.

"They abandoned him? Their flesh and blood?"

Gabe shook his head. "Alana kept track of his address, Josie. Mom told me last night that his mother has helped him with money from time to time."

Josie glared at him. "Your mother? You talked about this with your *mother* but not me?"

Aw, hell.

How to explain?

Gabe hadn't told her at first because he'd been reluctant to repeat gossip that might have been false.

He hadn't told her later because he'd feared that Joe would be as lazy as his mother had claimed. As foolish as Ella had insisted. Josie was the only person who'd opened her heart to a gentle man who'd made bad choices.

And in the end, Gabe hadn't told her because he'd been involved with her. He'd feared she would use it as an excuse to retreat. He had to face that now. Tell the gritty truth.

"I trusted you, Gabe."

"Josie, I swear I didn't make the connection until

after Earl gave us the name that night at Mary's. Then I didn't say anything because, well… I thought I needed to protect you. All I'd heard of Joe was that he didn't keep jobs and he drank any food money his mother gave him."

"You didn't trust me to find out for myself? Even if he lived under a cardboard box, that was my call."

He hadn't trusted her to find out. He should have. Josie was an adult, and more mature than Gabe in this way: she saw her father's weaknesses, but cherished his strengths.

Gabe had watched her respond to her father, and he'd fallen more deeply in love with her. And by the time he'd seen her openhearted acceptance of Joe, Gabe had felt that his confession would be too late.

Josie sprang from the chair and headed for the corridor. She exited through a side entrance and let herself into his car. All with him following.

Regretting.

They drove to Augusta in silence. Without asking where she wished to go, Gabe turned down the dirt road to her house. When she got out, he did, too. He walked her to the door. "May I step in for a minute?" he asked.

"I can't believe you'd ask."

She went inside without a smile, a look or a see-you-later. She closed the door behind herself before he'd even caught his breath.

HE SENT A humongous dang flower bouquet every day. Sometimes they arrived at her house, sometimes at her job. Now, on this Sunday afternoon in early February, they'd been delivered to Joe's house.

When she walked in to see the bouquet of white mums, gorgeous on the side table next to her father's chair, she laughed. "Oh, God. More white?"

Her father sat with a comforter over his lap. "I put them on the table so you'd see them right off," he said. "Guess he felt certain you'd visit here soon."

Gabe wasn't stupid. Her father had been released three days ago, and Gabe would recognize that Josie would want to check on him.

"Did you and Gabe have a falling out? You're coming and going at different times."

She lifted her chin and didn't answer. She'd noticed what her father had said. Gabe had been here to visit.

She couldn't restrain a twinge of affection.

Her father's mouth twisted. "He's a good guy, Josie-girl."

Josie plopped into the chair she'd added to her dad's living room. She reclined against the seat back and lifted her gaze to the ceiling. "He's not good for me, Dad."

"Why not?"

"He kept a secret from me."

"What secret?"

Josie bent forward, fussing with the comforter which covered her father's body. "You need anything? Hot tea? You hungry?"

"No, no and no." Joe waved away the very idea. "I want to hear this secret. It's about me, isn't it."

Crud.

Her father was no dummy, either. She might as well give him her side of the story. "Yes. You were the secret, okay? Gabe was aware of your connection to Alana a long time before I was." She shrugged. "He kept it from me."

"I didn't tell you about my family, either."

He hadn't.

Josie gave him a wry look. "But Gabe was supposed to be my best friend. I thought I could rely on him, above anyone, to be honest with me."

"Maybe he had a good reason to keep the secret."

"Like what?"

"Maybe he worried about what would happen if you found out. Maybe he was afraid you'd be hurt."

"Hah! That's just it. I'm a grown woman."

"Right. Then tell me this, Josie-girl. How can you forgive me? When your mother had another baby, I had suspicions." He paused. "But I allowed fear to prevent me from watching my own child grow up."

Josie could forgive her father because she accepted whatever she got from him, expecting little.

And thus, receiving a lot.

Joe bent forward, allowing the comforter to fall to his waist as he waited for a reply.

She couldn't reveal her every hurtful thought to her dad. Couldn't tell him her impressions of him as a man who'd bumbled his life, but who had strong points.

She had grown to love Joe. Her dad.

"Uh-huh," her father said, as if he could read her mind. "Don't let fear cheat you out of happiness, girl. I've lived my life alone. I don't recommend it."

Josie rolled her eyes and sighed. "I'm not afraid."

Her dad shoved the comforter completely aside, and

Josie was glad to note that he'd dressed in clean, new-looking jeans. He coughed once and sat back. "You worry about me, don't you?"

She held his gaze.

"Don't become like me."

Was that where she was headed? To a life as simple and lonely as her dad's?

He got up and plodded to his kitchen, and Josie followed. He filled a teakettle and set it over a burner. "That Gabriel Thomas loves you in a big way," he said with no hesitation. Just put it out there between them.

Her father turned the knob on the stove, then moved his gaze to the counter above Josie's head. "Grab a couple of cups, would you?"

She did, and as he accepted one he cackled. "Silly, isn't it? Some lonely old man giving you advice about love."

Josie smiled.

"I missed out on it. What is it that the players do in football?" he asked. "I fumbled it."

"Gabe's had you watching?"

"He thinks I should learn to enjoy it. He brings big, soft pretzels and root beer."

Now she laughed.

Her dad opened a tin to reveal some tea bags, took one and allowed Josie to select her own. "I fumbled it, Josie. I didn't know until you started coming here, but I missed having someone around." He tore open the paper wrapper, then nestled the bag in his cup. "I wasn't sure I deserved to be around anyone," he added quietly. "Because of my habits."

The teakettle sang.

Josie put a bag in her cup and waited for her father to pour the water. She yanked two new spoons from a drawer and they both stirred and sipped. The tea tasted herbal. Earthy.

Her dad winced.

"Why do you drink green tea if you don't like it?" she asked.

"I'm learning to like things that are better for me," he said. "I'm going to AA meetings over at the church, too. Did Gabe tell you that?"

Josie had her cup poised at her lips, but she brought it back down. Startled. "You are?"

"My mother invited me. She's ten years sober. She said she was waiting for the day I'd accept her help."

Josie attempted to blink back tears but gave up. They sprang from her face like some dang fountain. "That's great," she said.

"You okay?"

"Just happy."

He frowned into his cup.

Reacting to the pressure of her wishes, she thought.

Josie turned away from him to wipe her face and grab hold of her composure. As they finished their tea, they talked about Alana, her grandmother.

Thinking of her that way felt strange.

Alana had invited Joe to move in with her. Although she was healthy, she was nearing eighty. She said she'd appreciate the company, as long as Joe restricted his smoking to the outdoors. Or quit.

He was considering both suggestions.

An hour later, Josie returned home to her houseful of wilting white flowers. The answering machine light was blinking, so she set the mums next to it and pushed the button.

She felt a small disappointment when it wasn't Gabe's voice on the message, but she still grinned when she heard Isabel's feminine greeting. Izzy and Trevor had been on their way out with Darlene, but they had news.

She was pregnant again, due in October.

Josie was so happy for her. Isabel had been the closest to their mom. For Isabel to trust Trevor in the beginning must have taken an act of bravery. In a longtime marriage, maintaining that trust must require constant acts of faith and courage.

Josie felt an urge to call Gabe and tell him about the baby. He'd be excited, she was certain, but she wouldn't know how to start.

Sorry we haven't talked. I've always loved you a little too much, and I feared losing you?

Not at all brave. And just an excuse.

I'm sorry I was a jerk. Let's go to bed?

Brave, perhaps, but too much of the same old spiel.

And she also worried that Gabe wasn't asking for that much from her. He still wanted sex. Maybe he wasn't asking for sex from her forever.

He'd mentioned marriage once, but she'd viewed that as an attempt to keep going. She'd seen other guys use that ploy.

And if Gabe didn't want forever, why start up again?

Man, had she changed.

Valentine's Day fell on a Tuesday, and Josie found two dozen mixed roses on her step when she opened the door to get the paper. Two more bouquets had arrived at her job site before noon. None was white, however. They were reds, purples, yellows and pinks. Every bouquet was exquisite. Gabe must have spent a bundle. And every card said the same thing.

I won't stop loving you. Get used to this. Gabe.

It wasn't as witty as his earlier messages, but it had a similar effect. She yearned to welcome Gabe in her bed and her life for as long as possible.

Maybe she should try.

She drove straight to his house after work, and arrived at five-thirty. He might not be home yet, but she didn't care. She could wait.

She rang his doorbell, then heard the high whine of his jigsaw. He must be working in his garage.

She walked around to the side entrance and found him facing away from her at that workbench, wearing a big, dirty work suit and safety glasses.

He'd never looked sexier to her.

Josie watched him silently for a few minutes, as fascinated as always at the way he created something magnificent from a piece of raw material. Although Gabe had been contracting for years, he still adored getting his hands on the wood.

She loved that about him.

He cut a wide arc into a square of plywood, then blew the dust away and ran his finger over the curve.

An erotic image entered her thoughts, of him touching her that way on the same workbench.

When he shut off the saw, she cleared her throat.

Then again, more loudly.

Finally, he swivelled around.

"I came about the flowers."

He shoved his glasses onto his forehead and eyed her without smiling.

She ached for a smile.

"You made your point," she said. "You can stop."

He studied her, and she realized he was worried about what she'd say. About being hurt. That dear, big, wonderful man was worried that she would hurt him.

His tomboy friend, Josie.

Wow. She *could* hurt him, couldn't she?

He loved her that much.

She took a step forward. "So, are you still planning to die a bachelor?"

He shook his head, as if confused by the question.

"We've always said we'd get married only if we wanted kids, and we didn't because of the potential for inherited problems. We both said that, didn't we?"

She hesitated until he'd given a small nod, then she inched toward him again. "You realize there's a but, don't you?"

Were the corners of his mouth lifting?

"What we didn't realize then was that sometimes people marry because they love someone. There is reward in that lasting connection, don't you think?"

As she stepped within arm's reach of him, he gave her a bright look that took her breath away.

But she kept her cool, determined to tell him the rest.

"Shhh!" she said when he began to speak. Then,

"Gabe, I honestly believed that my sisters could make their relationships work because they were calm people. I considered myself too crazy to settle into marriage."

"And don't forget your marriage-is-boring mantra," he added, then shot a hot look from her head to her toes. "You are crazy, though." Slowly, he reached up and unzipped his body suit. When he had the zipper all the way down, he began peeling out of his clothes.

"Gabe!"

Now he shushed her, then kept stripping until he was bone-meltingly naked. "Bored?" he asked.

She didn't answer in words, but she was pretty certain he caught her meaning.

Later. Much, much later, when they'd loved their way through his house and up to that giant bathtub, he draped his arms around her shoulders from behind and whispered in her ear. "Just figured it all out, huh?"

"Something my dad said made me realize I was more afraid than angry. I kept finding excuses to back off."

"I thought that might be the case," Gabe said. "But I felt certain I could wait it out. You are braver than you realize, Josie. *And* more loving."

She was so glad she'd fallen in love with her best friend. "I've been keeping a secret from you, too."

She maneuvered around until her legs were looped over his. "I love you. In *that* way. Being in love with you is my normal, I guess."

A wonderfully pleased grin spread across his face. "Good."

He groped behind him to turn on the water spigot,

rewarming their cooling bath. Then he took her shoulders and drew her toward him, pausing for a moment to drip water onto her cleavage.

She laughed. "Do you have a thing about this bathtub, Gabe?"

"I have a thing about you." He kissed her for a while, then inched his lips away and murmured, "So, you wanna get married?"

A serious question. Hard to answer when he was nuzzling her neck. "What about the kids issue?" she asked. "You'd make a great dad, but we can't ignore the potential for problems."

He backed away and scowled. "We're talking about that now?"

She tittered. "Shouldn't we, Mr. Plan-Everything-Ahead?"

"If we decide we want them, there's adoption or genetic testing."

"Or, if it happens, would you mind if we just rattled around together for the next eighty years?" she asked.

He studied her again. "You plannin' to live past a hundred?"

She poked him in the ribs. "Aren't you?"

"Remember, I have a headstart." He slid near her again, claiming her mouth as he moved his hands to cup her bottom. The moment heated until Josie was ready for him.

But Gabe retreated this time. "Hey! Did you ever answer my question, Josie? About marrying me?"

"You just don't give up, do you?" she asked, sighing.

"Nope."

"Then, yes. Yes, I will."

"How's next week sound?"

It sounded perfect, but since Josie was more doer than talker, she showed him her answer this time.

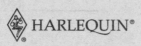

COMING NEXT MONTH

#1121 THE WYOMING KID by Debbie Macomber

What do you get when you mix an ex-rodeo cowboy who is used to being *mobbed* by adoring fans, and a sweet schoolteacher who is *not* interested in him? For Lonnie Ellison, formerly the Wyoming Kid, Joy Fuller's lack of interest is infuriating—and very appealing. This could be a match made in heaven! *Don't miss this guest appearance by the beloved* New York Times *bestselling author!*

#1122 COWBOY M.D. by Pamela Britton

Alison Forester won't take no for an answer, especially not from Dr. Nicholas Sheppard, the renowned reconstructive surgeon. Ali's driven by personal reasons to make the new burn unit at her hospital a success. But Nick has issues of his own, and he'd rather patch up rodeo cowboys than join Ali. Even if she isn't your average hospital administrator.

#1123 TO CATCH A HUSBAND by Laura Marie Altom

U.S. Marshals

U.S. Marshal Charity Caldwell's biological clock is tick, tick, ticking away, but the man she's loved *forever* thinks of her as nothing more than a friend. Charity's about at her breaking point when she launches a plan to help Adam Logue think of her as more than a friend, and even more than a woman—it's a plan to make him see she'll be the perfect wife!

#1124 AARON UNDER CONSTRUCTION by Marin Thomas

The McKade Brothers

Life had been handed to Aaron McKade on a silver platter—until his grandfather dared the pampered heir to get his hands dirty and take a job building houses in the barrio of south central L.A. That's when he traded his Italian loafers for steel-toed boots—and found a boss lady with a tool belt to "rebuild" him....

www.eHarlequin.com

HARCNM0606

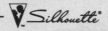

SPECIAL EDITION™

Welcome to Danbury Way— where nothing is as it seems...

Megan Schumacher has managed to maintain a low profile on Danbury Way by keeping the huge success of her graphics business a secret. But when a new client turns out to be a neighbor's sexy ex-husband, rumors of their developing romance quickly start to swirl.

THE RELUCTANT CINDERELLA

by CHRISTINE RIMMER

Available July 2006

Don't miss the first book from the Talk of the Neighborhood miniseries.

HOTEL MARCHAND

**Four sisters.
A family legacy.
And someone is out to destroy it.**

A captivating new limited continuity, launching June 2006

The most beautiful hotel in New Orleans,
and someone is out to destroy it. But mystery,
danger and some surprising family revelations
and discoveries won't stop the Marchand sisters
from protecting their birthright…
and finding love along the way.

SPECIAL PRICE!

This riveting new saga begins with

In the Dark

by national bestselling author

JUDITH ARNOLD

The party at Hotel Marchand is in full swing when the lights suddenly go out. What does head of security Mac Jensen do first? He's torn between two jobs—protecting the guests at the hotel and keeping the woman he loves safe.

A woman to protect. A hotel to secure. And no idea who's determined to harm them.

On Sale June 2006

**Hidden in the secrets of antiquity,
lies the unimagined truth...**

Introducing

a brand-new line filled with mystery
and suspense, action and adventure,
and a fascinating look into history.
And it all begins with DESTINY.

In a sealed crypt in
France, where the
terrifying legend of
the beast of Gevaudan
begins to unravel,
Annja Creed discovers
a stunning artifact
that will seal her destiny.

*Available every other
month starting
July 2006, wherever
you buy books.*

Page-turning drama…

Exotic, glamorous locations…

Intense emotion and passionate seduction…

Sheikhs, princes and billionaire tycoons…

This summer, may we suggest:

THE SHEIKH'S DISOBEDIENT BRIDE
by Jane Porter
On sale June.

AT THE GREEK TYCOON'S BIDDING
by Cathy Williams
On sale July.

THE ITALIAN MILLIONAIRE'S VIRGIN WIFE
On sale August.

With new titles to choose from every month,
discover a world of romance in our books written
by internationally bestselling authors.

HARLEQUIN® *Presents*

It's the ultimate in quality romance!

Available wherever Harlequin books are sold.

www.eHarlequin.com

HPGEN06

If you enjoyed what you just read,
then we've got an offer you can't resist!

Take 2 bestselling
love stories FREE!
Plus get a FREE surprise gift!

Clip this page and mail it to Harlequin Reader Service®

IN U.S.A.
3010 Walden Ave.
P.O. Box 1867
Buffalo, N.Y. 14240-1867

IN CANADA
P.O. Box 609
Fort Erie, Ontario
L2A 5X3

YES! Please send me 2 free Harlequin American Romance® novels and my free surprise gift. After receiving them, if I don't wish to receive anymore, I can return the shipping statement marked cancel. If I don't cancel, I will receive 4 brand-new novels every month, before they're available in stores! In the U.S.A., bill me at the bargain price of $4.24 plus 25¢ shipping & handling per book and applicable sales tax, if any*. In Canada, bill me at the bargain price of $4.99 plus 25¢ shipping & handling per book and applicable taxes**. That's the complete price and a savings of at least 10% off the cover prices—what a great deal! I understand that accepting the 2 free books and gift places me under no obligation ever to buy any books. I can always return a shipment and cancel at any time. Even if I never buy another book from Harlequin, the 2 free books and gift are mine to keep forever.

154 HDN DZ7S
354 HDN DZ7T

Name	(PLEASE PRINT)	
Address	Apt.#	
City	State/Prov.	Zip/Postal Code

Not valid to current Harlequin American Romance® subscribers.

Want to try two free books from another series?
Call 1-800-873-8635 or visit www.morefreebooks.com.

* Terms and prices subject to change without notice. Sales tax applicable in N.Y.
** Canadian residents will be charged applicable provincial taxes and GST.
All orders subject to approval. Offer limited to one per household.
® are registered trademarks owned and used by the trademark owner and or its licensee.

AMER04R   ©2004 Harlequin Enterprises Limited